NIGHT TRAFFIC

Urban tales

by

Bruce Harris

The Conrad Press

Night Traffic
Published by The Conrad Press in the United
Kingdom 2024
Tel: +44(0)1227 472 874
www.theconradpress.com
info@theconradpress.com
ISBN 978-1-916966-59-8
Typesetting and Cover Design by: Levellers
The Conrad Press logo was designed by Maria
Priestley.
Printed and bound in Great Britain by Clays Ltd,
Elcograf S.p.A.

For my sister, Christine Anne Medd,
on a significant birthday

Contents:

NIGHT TRAFFIC

A big Audi glides underground beneath the impressive Victorian façade of a five-star London hotel. In the faded yellow light of the car park, it creeps tentatively down a lane parallel to the hotel's basement until the driver sees a figure in a concierge uniform waving him into a reserved space. Thirty yards inside an unobtrusive rear entrance, the manager Paul Kendall, a spare, dark man in his late thirties and a faultless blue suit, watches carefully as the car glides majestically to a halt and four people emerge almost immediately.

From the front passenger seat, a muscular African American man called Chester Mayfield moves behind the car to the right side back door, which he opens. Chester is a modern bodyguard, with muscle but technology too, as the gadget in his right hand is telling him exactly how many human forms are in his immediate vicinity. Over-enthusiastic fans, paparazzi low-life, would-be terrorists, Chester doesn't like unpleasant surprises.

From back left seat, another big man gets out, though this time the build is more tall and lean. Dan Shaw is East End, worldly wise and unimpressed, his expression inscrutable while his darting eyes register every detail of his surroundings. He too deplores surprises.

The driver, a Russian who answers to Leo, is admonishing the concierge in clipped, abrupt English for what he perceives as inadequate directions when a curt remark in Russian from the lady behind him cuts him short. She emerges from the car with the careful elegance bred from a lifetime of celebrity.

Marianne Chine, christened Mariya Chinelnitsky, is fifty-six years old, but her natural tan, expensively-maintained smooth complexion and clear, challenging blue eyes make her look ten years younger. She has shortened her dark hair to an almost boyish cut, partly to hide the occasional strands of grey. At close quarters, her age shows more clearly in lines bordering the eyes and mouth.

Marianne sees herself as an Englishwoman, even if bilingual from her mother's conscientious Russian instruction. She is in London because she has again been nominated for a BAFTA and the award ceremony is two days away. Having been nominated without result twice before, she has decided she needs preparation time before going through the whole crazy shindig all over again.

She also has a clandestine side to her activities which makes a secure location desirable, and she sees the hotel as a London safe house, because of its trustworthy management. Nevertheless, she has her U.S. and U.K. bodyguards with her for extra insurance, as well as Leo, with whom she talks Russian when, for whatever reason, she only wants him to know what she is saying. Leo, like Russia, preserves a useful if back row position in her life.

Her late grandparents, in their childhood years, accompanied their parents from the Ukraine to the East End of London after another pogrom laid waste Jewish lives and properties, and with typical resource, their business as guides for show business foreigners in London proved gratifyingly lucrative. The emergence of a grandchild who was talented enough as a performer to be both client and relative was a delightful bonus in their later years.

6

Marianne crosses the fifteen yards to the hotel door as rapidly as age and stardom allows and her men gather around her in a protective phalanx. Only when they are all standing in the lobby area with the outside door locked behind them does she throw her arms around the waiting Kendall and kiss his cheek lightly.

'Paul, bless you. As smooth as ever. Shut UP, Leo. I used to love London; now the traffic frightens me, so fast and unforgiving,' she said, her eyes remaining on the young manager's welcoming smile even as she snaps at her driver.

'It's wonderful to have you here again, Marianne,' the manager says, his flush showing more than formal courtesy. 'We have your suite ready. All phone calls will be vetted; if you need to send out e-mails, call me. We'll make sure you have peace enough to prepare yourself, Marianne, and we're all rooting for you to make it third time lucky.'

'Thank you, Paul. You know, this is one of the few London places where I feel secure. How old do I have to be before they get their noses out of my life? I'm a wealthy woman, but sometimes I feel imprisoned in these cities.'

As they approach the lift going up to the Carlton Suite, Paul holds up his hand on the edge of the public corridor to check on people passing. Marianne and her entourage pause, and she glances across to the ornate cocktail bar, all golden gilt and immense mirrors. At this angle, she can see without being seen, and for a few seconds, she watches the single customer, an exquisitely beautiful blonde-haired girl who cannot possibly be older than her early twenties; Marianne knows when youth has no need for disguise. Framed in an enormous armchair, the girl's pale face and partly exposed shoulders hint at real fragility and vulnerability.

Just before her party are beckoned on, Marianne also recognises in the girl the stiff dignity of the exile out of her depth in a foreign country, with perhaps something of eastern European pride. A familiar alert forms itself in her mind.

Installed in the fussy splendour of the Carlton Suite, a stately confection of scarlet carpets and extravagant dark wood furniture, with Chester and Dan outside testily working out a door-guarding rota, Marianne and Paul have coffee. She loves the way Paul makes time for her, in spite of his highly demanding job.

'How's Claudio?' Paul says dutifully, though he knows the reputation of Marianne's third husband and the ludicrously well-publicised problems of their marriage.

'Oh, screwing his way around Beverley Hills as usual, I should think,' Marianne answers dismissively. 'It doesn't worry me now, Paul. I'd divorce, but there's no way I'm letting those piranha lawyers feed in my trough all over again. And when he's with his current floozie, he's not bothering me. And Jane?'

'Doing very well,' Paul says, too enthusiastically. 'She has a stable of musicians and artists on her books now, and it's endless exhibitions and performances. We meet each other *en passant* from time to time.'

Marianne thinks his tone more eloquent than his words, but she is too tired to probe deeply. She takes one of his hands and squeezes it with a friendliness which could be consolation if it needs to be. Then she adopts a brisker tone.

'Now, Paul, it's sweet of you to chat with me for a while, but I know what it takes to run this hotel. I'm quite tired in any case. But, tell me, just out of my nosiness. Who was that lovely girl sitting in the bar all on her own?'

He glances distractedly away and she misinterprets the movement.

8

'No problem; if it's confidential, of course –'

'No,' he says, with a touch of embarrassment. 'In this case, it's not confidential, Marianne. She's in a public place. It's just one of those sticky situations that happen in this business.'

'Oh?'

'They check in, her and a big guy, supposedly her husband. He's built like a prize-fighter, but he's always very proper; civilised, well-dressed. It's only in his eyes and glances that you see a guy you wouldn't want to meet down a dark alley, if you know what I mean.'

'Yes, oh, yes. I'm in showbiz; they gather like wolves, normally in the pay of men even worse than they are. I know the species very well.'

'He fronts as an investment manager; he makes sure no-one is any doubt about it. He says he's in London from the States to see people, do business, make deals. His wife gets very bored with meetings and all the finance talk, he says, so she relaxes in the safe environment of the hotel bar and occasionally asks her friends to come to her, and maybe take her somewhere nice.'

'Seems straightforward, Paul.'

'Sure. But most of the time her friends are male, and they don't always come across convincingly as long-standing buddies. And we know that sometimes she and the lucky guy – always married men - go off to an apartment where he has his fun in front of hidden cams so he can be threatened with it afterwards. The victims don't call in the police because they can't prove anything, or they can't remember the place, or they're spooked by the threats. Judging by a few anonymous calls I've had, some of them think the hotel is in on it. The pimp pays for his room in advance. I suspect they're using my hotel to run a high-class extortion deal.'

'Don't take the bookings. Tell him the place is full. Ban him.'

'On what grounds, Marianne? Nothing happens here except the pick-up, but I can't even prove that conclusively. Even if I did ban him, he would work in another company's name, or book a room in another name; I can't down the whole booking system because of him. Plus she looks too classy to be a hooker. I suspect she hasn't been doing it for very long. Chances are they'll move on soon and leave us in peace. But don't be concerned, Marianne; I've been here before. I'll think of something. I usually do; it's why I'm still here.'

He smiles and gets quickly to his feet.

'Just a minute, Paul.'

He sits down again and she sees a small flush on his cheek as she leans towards him.

'Now, don't take this like an attack on all mankind, Paul, but I've been with Chester, Dan and Leo for a while and they're great guys, but the testosterone crackles around me like a wind trap and female company tonight is something I could appreciate. Ask that lonely girl if she'll join me for a drink before she goes wherever she's going. She didn't look as if she's waiting for a guy yet, and even if she is, he can wait while she talks to a movie star. Feather in her cap. Who wouldn't? Just tell her that a megastar wants girlie company for half an hour. I've been around a while, Paul. I'll get the measure of her and we'll take it from there.

What do you think?'

In the time it takes Marianne to drink half a glass of restorative champagne, a knock so quiet as to be almost inaudible lands on her door. She finds Paul in the corridor, with the girl beside him, looking even more beautiful when not being observed in her unhappiness.

Paul backs away with a smile, a guy who knows when words are unnecessary, and the girl comes into the room.

Yes, she is stunning, and unusually, even more so at close quarters, Marianne thinks. Her effort to retain her cool might seem a little too studied, but she probably doesn't meet a movie star every day of the week, even an old stager like Madame Chine. She offers the girl a flute of champagne and it is taken with a quiet smile, as if only to be expected. Marianne sits on her favourite armchair and the girl poses herself, literally, at the end of the nearest sofa, her sky blue eyes remaining carefully fixed on Marianne.

'Let's get acquainted, darling, as they say in L.A. I'm Mari-'

'Oh, I know who you are, Miss Chine. I know what you've been nominated for this time, the BBC series The Last Tsarina, Tsarina Alexandra, friend of Rasputin, murdered by the Bolsheviks. I thought you were wonderful in it. You simply must win this time.'

Marianne smiles; all just a little too well thought out, almost rehearsed. And while the accent is difficult to identify, it is an accent. Little buzzers of familiarity are sounding in her mind from a past not as blameless as her publicity now made it. Her recent parts were well known, and even when they weren't, the information could be googled.

The girl was trained to please whoever she needed to please – forced, Marianne would bet on it, to please - and the older woman marvelled at the contrast between such delicate, ethereal beauty and the parallel determination to agree and flatter at every turn. Her name is Eva, though even she doesn't seem very familiar with it.

At one point, she puts one hand lightly on Marianne's knee; at another, she lowers her eyes and gives Marianne a look to make clear that her repertoire isn't necessarily restricted to heterosexuality if something else is on the cards. Marianne contemplates how the watchers would enjoy the girl on girl action should she be tempted to 'go visit my place,' if that invitation is about to come down the line. And if gay was me, Marianne thought, this lovely would certainly be me as well. Her beauty is stunning and has a natural quality about it; Paul is probably right to say she hasn't been doing what she is doing for long.

As she watches the girl set herself out to be charming, Marianne begins to see her younger self where the girl was, remembering an old actress from many years ago. After a stellar early career, the lady in question had landed a regular part in a long-running soap opera – 'got to keep the wolf from the door, darling; most of my glories faded a while back.'

Marianne remembers her in her small television dressing room, slouched towards the mirror doing her own make-up. Her agent managed to get Marianne a cameo part in the same soap, and paying respects to the old stager was a matter of simple etiquette.

Marianne stuttered through her praise lines while the making-up process continued. Finally, the lady turned to face her young admirer head on.

She didn't comment on Marianne's fulsome comments, a reaction Marianne herself grew to understand in time. For a while, nothing was said, while the older woman studied the younger before her.

'You are quite beautiful, even at close quarters, my dear.'

'Thank you,' said Marianne. 'I think. I'm never sure what to say. I suppose I should be thankful, but then it hasn't got much to do with me.'

Carole – Marianne finally remembered the name – turned back to her mirror.

'Don't be too thankful. Beauty is a gilded cage, darling. Luxurious surroundings, adulation, good times, expensive clothes, all of that. But a cage all the same, and usually men are the captors and keyholders.

When your beauty goes, you will find yourself, like me, making these ludicrous cosmetic attempts to preserve whatever's left. But you will be free. The woman I play in this everlasting saga is a snake-tongued old harridan, to be sure, but she is vastly more interesting as a part than the love interest I always used to get saddled with, sitting in my cage tweeting decorously. 'Oh, sir, how can you say so? I'm sure you are the very epitome of bravery and duty'.'

She turned to Marianne again and fluttered her eyelashes. Marianne burst out laughing, but the lady's words stayed with her for always. She remembered them again when accepting the part of Tsarina Alexandra, a woman in her fifties playing a woman in her forties, yes, but enough beauty still lingered to make it credible with suitable cosmetic assistance, and the Tsarina had so many nuances about her royal person that the part was probably just as fascinating as Carole's snake-tongued old harridan, if not in the same way.

Carole had been right; the parts gathered interest value as the years went by, and her sense is, as she gazes upon the exquisite young woman before her, that the gilded cage is where this girl is living. The acting profession is about adopting other identities, and she sees another woman behind the ill-fitting facade, a being suppressed and hidden almost to oblivion, but not quite. She keeps the small talk going long enough to garnish information. Having bided her time, she eventually decides on tactics.

13

She waits until the girl is taking her leave. After they hug and the girl walks, still with her studied coolness, towards the door, Marianne breaks into Russian.

'Where are you from, child? Moldova, Romania, the Ukraine? Who is this man who runs your life? What hold does he have over you?'

The girl stands still, frozen into uncertainty, as if knowing she should run out and finding herself unable to do so. Marianne continues in Russian.

'It isn't the way it needs to be, my darling. You don't have to do his bidding – in this hotel, or any other. Trust me, Eva. Please.'

Eva replies in a different tone, deep and quiet, in the accented Russian of Moldova.

'What do you know of it, old woman? You want to be my mother? Keep your prying Ivan nose out of my business.'

Marianne sits down and turns her face unhappily away, trying to think of alternative plans now that the situation is clear. She waits for the door to click and reaches for consolation champagne.

But the click never comes. She turns to see the girl, her hand frozen on the door handle, dissolve suddenly into uncontrollable tears. Marianne gently detaches the hand and leads her back to the sofa.

'I must please whoever takes an interest, he says. I must do whatever I am bid, or my beauty will not see another year. I believe him. I have seen what he has done to other girls.'

The whole story soon emerges; the application for a job as a 'personal assistant'; the delight of Iana, the girl's real name, and her family at her success; the long trek from Moldova to Istanbul, where she meets supposed representatives of her prospective employers; the arrival in London and immediate confinement to a house for

14

'induction,' which means having personal possessions, money and papers stolen and being told very directly what was expected of her. Her campaign of strategic obedience has won her way to being the 'personal assistant' of her 'supervisor' Raoul, whose exact nationality or identity she still doesn't know.

By abasing herself to such an extent that 'my pride drains from me and all I have is hope,' she has won enough trust from Raoul to become his partner in hotel stings, where she entices wealthy men to an equipped apartment to be placed on cam 'doing what they did'; the girl's shudder makes Marianne throw her arms impulsively around her.

When Raoul and his companions appear, the threats of exposure are usually enough; violence is rarely necessary. When it is, Raoul 'minimises the disturbance' with gags, covers and closed doors. She understands that anything less than total obedience on her part will rapidly subject her to similar treatment, though she feels Raoul has as much liking for her as he is capable of feeling, and she has been given back her passport in case of hotel queries.

But making a break for an airport still wasn't feasible, because she has no other papers and no money beyond a cash supply for a single night. Going to the police was too great a risk, because if they didn't believe her or took time checking her story, she would be dead or maimed within a day. Similarly the Moldovan Embassy; Raoul has convincing paperwork concerning her supposed employment; she only has the passport.

Marianne walks around her suite thinking, while Iana, exhausted by revelation, sips champagne on the sofa, holding the glass before her like a trophy and rocking slowly backwards and forwards. Marianne is used to thinking on her feet, in both her open and concealed working lives.

'Listen, honey,' she says eventually. 'Both of us are prisoners in this city; the difference is that I have an escape route and you haven't. This is what I suggest we do. I've got a place in the far south-west of England that nobody knows about but two close friends in the same organisation as myself. It's kept for me by a sweet couple – the lady is my cousin. Without it, I think I would have gone crazy sometimes.

I suggest I send you down there later on tonight, with Leo; Leo is a good driver, and he speaks Russian if you need to say something you don't want anyone to understand. I can get a private message to Sonya and Michael in Devon. When you've had a few days to start getting this city out of your system, I'll join you after the BAFTA jamboree, because I'll have to cool down myself by then, win or lose.

Then we'll talk to people; I have contacts in Unseen U.K., the Human Trafficking Foundation, Women's Aid. We'll give them chapter and verse, and start tracking the bastards down. I do this stuff now, but on the quiet, because I don't want more journalists around my neck. What do you say?'

Iana's answer at first is more tears and a clutch at the older woman's hand.

'But what will happen when Raoul comes? You don't know him, Marianne. He could tear this place apart.'

'Not with Chester and Dan around, honey, he couldn't. Not to mention the hotel security guys; I know the manager, and he's nobody's fool. And anyway, I have a plan in mind. He lets you go off with these strange guys – God, Iana, any one of them could be a homicidal freak; does he really care about you, darling? Leave that. All we

16

have to do is persuade him that you left the hotel; we've got security cameras for that.'

'And this?' says Iana, taking a sleek black phone from her coat. 'He has a tracker on it.'

'We'll give that to Chester. He knows what to do with them. It'll be stone dead. And once the people I know get working on it, we'll have a tracker on him.'

Paul comes to the suite later, and after several relevant questions, he agrees with the scheme, to rid himself and the hotel of Raoul and his works as well as helping Iana.

At twenty minutes to ten, security cameras record Iana leaving on Dan's arm and getting into an unmarked car. Dan takes them on a circuitous half hour journey while watching out for any signs of the car being followed. He looks across at Iana at one point, and sees the fear in her eyes. Dan smiles and winks.

'Nothing's going to happen to you tonight, girl; you just be sure of that.'

'It's as it was when I came into this city, full of hope and optimism. It seemed like a brilliant new world. Since then, it has come to mean just going to or coming from yet another –'

Dan shakes his head.

'Big cities are the biggest cons of all,' he says. 'Flashing colours, big windows, endless opportunities. As many nightmares as promises.'

With Dan confident that nothing had followed them, the car draws up at a delivery bay at the back of the hotel, and re-enters at a pre-arranged point not covered by cameras. At 22.25, a little party gather at the door leading to the underground car park where Marianne had entered earlier in the day.

'Leo's going to take you to Devon, Iana, love,' Marianne says. 'No detours. Stretch out on the back seat

17

and sleep until the London night is gone and all you'll see is the country passing by. Sonya and Michael have been working with me for some time, and they won't be asking awkward questions. They'll take good care of you, darling. See you in a week.'

At 23.30, Raoul Alvirez enters the hotel foyer; he towers over the companions beside him. His mouth is set in a thin, straight line; his dark eyes are hard and unmoving. The hotel receptionist, Rachel, carefully presses a button under her desk.

'Room 557. Has my wife returned to the hotel?' Alvirez says.

'I don't know, sir. I think she was in the bar earlier on.'

When he comes down from the room, the eyes have taken on a murderous gleam. This time, Paul stands to face him.

'You seem concerned, Mr. Alvirez. Can I help?'

Something of Raoul's savoir faire returns, and he manages a bleak smile.

'It is true my wife sometimes goes out; she has friends in London. But she should certainly have returned by now. Her things have gone. I am a little anxious.'

This is the only man he knows, Paul thinks, who can make a threat of the word 'anxious.' He makes himself look concerned.

'If you wish it, Mr. Alvirez, we will check the security cameras to see if and when Mrs. Alvirez left the hotel.'

Alvirez's expression speaks of a suspicion made more acute by its lack of focus. Paul can see the conflict in him, a violent nature forced to moderation. He offers Alvirez a complementary drink 'to ease your anxiety' while the footage is being checked; the big man's eyes narrow with contempt for the idea that he should need a drink, but he goes, shoulders swaying, his walk resembling a big, predatory cat, the eyes calmly searching for anything he might wish to devour.

Paul knows where the footage is, but he delays for a credible interval before summoning Alvirez into the back office, showing him the unmistakable figure of Eva opening the main hotel doors. Dan's back is towards the entrance; Eva puts her arm into his as soon as she is on the steps outside, and they get into the car without a glance behind them. The time – 21.38 – is indicated quite clearly on the screen.

Alvirez is about to say something; Paul gets in first.

'We have no idea who her companion was, sir, I'm afraid. This is a hotel; I'm afraid we

cannot control our guests' comings and goings.'

For a long, long moment, the two men's eyes meet, and Alvirez's companions imitate their master's cold stare. Paul judges that Alvirez is suspicious and intensely violent by nature, and his whole demeanour speaks deep unease about what is happening. At this moment, Chester casually enters the office with two hotel security staff, and thirty long seconds pass silently while both sides sum up each other. To Paul's intense relief, Alvirez suddenly turns on his heel and bangs out of the office and the hotel, while already clicking at his phone.

When Paul confirms to her that Alvirez has left the hotel and almost certainly wouldn't be coming back, Marianne treats herself to a soak in the bath. She knows, from her private line to Leo, that he and Iana are already half way to Devon. Iana isn't the first trafficked girl Marianne and her helpers have spirited away, and Marianne remains determined she won't be the last. That beautiful, lonely figure in the bar set her alarm bells ringing immediately.

Her activities remain unknown, as far as she can tell, from the media. They explain why she employs bodyguards who aren't just bodyguards and drivers who aren't just drivers. It remains vital that she keeps her actions hidden, both for the sake of the escaping girls and the chances of continuing success. She could remember one of her teachers, a scientist, describing acting as 'pointless,' but there were occasions when the point was only too clear, particularly when she had saved her own or someone else's life with it.

Finally stretching out in the warmth and splendour of her suite's bathroom, Marianne reflects on the lofty contempt of her idealistic younger self for money and those obsessed with the pursuit of it. 'Just remember, Marianne,' she could remember her exasperated father saying, 'money is power. Yes, some people waste it on self-indulgence, but it doesn't have to be like that; there are also good uses for it. With none at all, you haven't even got the choice, have you?'

'No, Dad,' she could remember saying, as she nodded dutifully and wondered what he was talking about. But one memorable day, she got to talking, really talking, with Grandmother Valentina, when the old woman knew she was dying. Marianne heard how it was to cower in the night from the Jew-haters, in dwellings that offered only flimsy protection, listening in the small hours for tiny noises which might build into huge, menacing invasions.

'When those noises build to a crescendo,' Valentina said, fighting for breath, 'there is nothing left but to clutch together and pray to whatever you have persuaded yourself to believe in. Your choices are that or total despair.'

Marianne found herself identifying so thoroughly with her grandmother's girlhood that she was propelled towards taking acting seriously rather than toying with it. Even the experiences of the Tsarina, one of the most powerful women in the world until she found herself cowering with her entire family in a six metres by five cellar in Yekaterinburg, listening for those noises, could be rendered as understandable as the old Jewish woman in a pogrom. The successful Marianne found herself able to think into both the woman's power and glory as well as her eventual downfall.

She shuts her eyes and sinks down into the water, intimidated by such memories of night terrors even in her ultra-secure hotel suite, when an image comes to her of Iana in the car taking her to a new life. For once, the night traffic in Iana's life will be benign, the city will become rural peace, the predatory beasts and monsters will fade behind her and, eventually, she will see the coast, the gulls, the easy murmur of waves and an ocean of new life waiting on the doorstep.

Marianne opens her eyes, rests her head on the back of the bath, and smiles.

NIGHTCAPS FOR WILD BOYS

The Don in Don's All-Nite Diner is me, but it doesn't have to be me in it at half past four in the morning, staring out of the front windows like a spaceman peering out of his spaceship into the void, two grey dim squares in the dawn light. People sometimes turn their pale faces in my direction like puzzled ghosts, though more often they will hurry past, heads bowed, as if pursued by some mystery of the night.

Marie, my wife, doesn't understand why I still do some night shifts.

'You don't need to bother now, Don,' she says. 'We're comfortable enough.' It's a fair point, letting myself sink gently into the easy middle age I've worked for. But pragmatic, real-world Marie doesn't see the fascinations of the small hours, and some of the valued contacts and friends I've developed over the years.

No phantoms, werewolves, axe wielding murderers. Not around these parts anyway. Most of them are in one of three groups; firstly, the insomniacs who have long since had enough of lying in darkened rooms staring at walls. They suffer for all sorts of reasons – unbalanced work shifts, anxieties, nagging conditions like tinnitus or unresolved aches and pains. Occasionally, grief and mercifully rarely, despair.

Then there are the hospital workers, the nearby hospital being one of the reasons the place exists. Usually it's going on or knocking off shifts which brings them in. Sure, there are places to eat and drink in the hospital, but Eileen, a senior nurse about to go on a Saturday night shift to deal with the usual supply of people off their face on drinks or drugs or both, summed up the diner to me.

'You wind yourself up to go into the hospital, Don, and you wind yourself down when you come out. In there is a place where rules and words are not the same, where literally anything can happen and sometimes it does. You need normality before you go in and normality when you come out.'

They're in here, some of them scarcely more than kids, pop eyed with tiredness or shock, struggling to come to terms with the things they've seen or had to do. My diner is their pre-battle tent and post-battle camp fire.

And then, of course, there are the wild boys, and it is usually boys, perhaps because girls have too much to lose to wonder about aimlessly in the small hours. The boys and their testosterone are on an endless rootless hunt for something, excitement, danger, sex, whatever. They arrive on the neck ends of stag nights or booze ups, boys up to their mid and late twenties too far gone to risk going home – a surprising number of them still live at home – or with nothing to do after they've missed buses and can't afford taxis. Sometimes it's aftermaths of fights, when they don't want to get mixed up with officialdom, running risk of losing jobs or being banged up in a young offenders' place. And perhaps there's a certain genetic devilry which comes from countless generations of being sent off to war as soon as they're old enough to use a weapon.

Mostly they don't start anything on my premises, because word gets around the wild boys about where the small hours' safe places are, who are friends or enemies or bits of both, and they're usually not far from manhood by the time they get to distinguish the third. I won't take nonsense from them, but I won't shop them either; it establishes a kind of trust.

23

Of course, I take precautions; I didn't get this far – Don's Diner isn't my only establishment – by being naïve. I have alarm buttons to the police under my side of the serving counter. The door to the office and stock room behind the main cafe is solid metal and locks easily if any staff need to get behind it. The place has an anti-fire sprinkler system which can serve other purposes if it needs to; the entrance door and the windows on either side of it can be locked and shuttered in a matter of seconds. People who run catering places are always moaning about the costs of security, but they find themselves moaning even more if their place is wrecked and insurance is fighting them because of inadequate precautions.

And the wild boys know all this stuff. Wild they may be; mad they're not. The wildness is qualified; it's still related to teenage tantrums and exploring what you can get away with, and it remembers who is and isn't impressed by tantrums. Officialdom might not be so savage in dealing with them as it once was, but the big wide world can still be and often is. I've had small hours visits from boys who've picked the wrong bouncer to start something with, or run into boys tougher than them, or come up against vehicles, doors or other solid forms which don't move out of the way just because a wild boy wants them to. My place can be their young adult equivalent of running upstairs and locking themselves in their rooms.

My first dawn visitor on this shift is one of the insomniacs. It's Maggie Pierce once more, looking wasted even by her standards, her face pale and her eyes ringed with wrinkles of fatigue, but doing her best to smile as if she hasn't seen me for twenty years.

'Wide awake again, Don,' she says, edging her way across to a side table; I never have seen Maggie head in a straight line towards the counter. It's as if she's consigned herself so much to the periphery of the world that it even translates into where she physically places herself.

'Coffee?' I say. It's illogical, of course, for insomniacs to drink coffee; it's coffee which made many of them insomniac in the first place, but most of them still drink it.

'Sod it, yes,' she says. 'If I can't have what I need, I might as well have what I want.'

I take her coffee over to her – Maggie's is black and sugarless, so it doesn't take long – and as I close in on her, an alarm bell has already started letting out a few warning rings. She always is pale; now she's just too pale, on the borderline of a kind of death pallor. Something has frightened her quite badly, and Maggie is a habitual dawn wanderer, she doesn't take fright that easily. Her eyes are often downcast, with intermittent blinking as if repeatedly surprised, but now they look truly despairing, as though she's finally seen something in the grey light which she just can't take.

I sit down beside her and place a hand briefly on her arm. She gives me another attempt at a beamer which flickers and dies in a second, and then she digs down into her coat pocket and brings out a bottle of pills. Putting them down on the table as if a conclusive exhibit of something, she looks at me and my face forms my question.

'I've spent two hours tonight with them spread out on a table before me, Don. Five minutes, I thought, is all it would take, and then I could finally know, really know, whether there's anything better than this, or whether there's nothing at all, and if it's something better, it wouldn't be difficult, and if it's nothing at all, I wouldn't need to worry anyway, would I?'

I've known Maggie long enough to recognise her pills; they're powerful sleeping pills, about the nearest things to knockouts you can legally get. They are available on prescription, but whether any doctor would supply someone like Maggie with the sort of numbers in this bottle, I doubt, which makes me wonder where and who she gets them from.

Maggie used to be in the catering business herself, if you can call a pub that. She worked in the hospital for a while as a nurse, and was thinking of doing something else when she met a barman called Tony in a pub. He told her he wanted to set up a pub of his own, with some inherited money, and that's what they did; they married, and Maggie put what money she had into their venture alongside his. At the time, she was happy to leave nursing, which she was finding hugely draining, both physically and mentally. Tony turned into a drunk, and she found herself dealing with his lock ins with his mates; their only son Malcolm lost all patience with Tony in his late teens and left to live with a mate before moving away from the area altogether. Tony drank himself into a fatal heart attack, and Maggie was left with a pub she no longer had the heart to keep going. She made enough from the sale to buy a decent flat and provide herself with a small income, which she fills out with bar work. She also works in the Friends of the Hospital coffee shop, but that's voluntary.

All sounding pretty hopeless, I suppose, and even more so when she's sat there, moist and doe-eyed, talking about doing away with herself. But Maggie is still a gutsy, funny, observer of people, popular in the hospital and happy to spend hours talking to people about life, love and the pursuit of happiness, all of which she knows a good deal about.

There we both are, staring at this little bottle as if it's about to do a tap dance, and suddenly a cracked, raucous bellow sounds from down the street, so obviously emanating from a wild boy that it could serve as a kind of signature tune.

'Yes,' says Maggie, as if remembering a detail, 'there are some boys in the street. I heard one of them shouting at me as I went by.'

And her eyes flicker back to the bottle as her body flinches from it, and I see that wild boys don't really frighten Maggie; what frightens Maggie is Maggie, and especially a Maggie seriously contemplating doing away with herself. For all that she's been through, you'd think the idea might have occurred to her before; the fact that it never has is symptomatic of her strength, not her weakness. No wonder she's so frightened. Nothing is so terrifying as rebellion from within, when you look for support and find betrayal.

Another animalistic screech and a scuffed kick, closer this time. I come to a decision.

'Maggie, come through to the back. Here, I'll bring your coffee.'

The area behind the main café is divided into two, on the left the stockroom for non-perishables, crockery, cutlery, etc., with the big freezer behind them. On the right is a smaller area, with a coffee table and a couple of easy chairs, which Marie regards as our inner sanctum, where we can take our ease when it's not so busy and leave the staff to get on with it. Marie would probably concede that a suicidal customer is a fair exception.

'There now, Maggie love. Sit there where it's peaceful; leave the boys to me.'

I pick up the pill bottle and put it in my pocket.

'I'm going to hold on to these, my darling, for a bit. When we get the chance, we'll talk.'

27

On an impulse, I go to the drinks cabinet and pour her a decent shot of brandy.

'Get that down you now. Back in a minute,' I say, and almost simultaneously, the café door crashes open and there they are. I shut the door behind me and walk through to the front. There are three of them; one tall youth, with dark, simian features, swaying and looking around him as if he's landed on an alien planet; a stocky, blondish boy, clean shaven and currently with his hands stuck deep in his pockets as he swallows, trying, I suspect, not to be sick. The third lad I know – there's always at least one I know - Joe Lytham, one of those wiry, elastic kids who looks as if a strong wind could blow him away but could graft all day and fight all night if he had a mind to, and every now and then, he does. He actually has a good apprenticeship in a tool-making place, but the urge to walk on the wild side now and then is still sometimes irresistible.

'Don,' he says, putting his long sinewy arm around my neck and breathing booze at me. He turns to his friends.

'This is my mate Don, boys. Remember that time we met up with those fucking Field brothers and their mates; remember that?'

The blond boy resumes swallowing; he has trouble speaking, and something tells me he doesn't know where he is or what he's doing, apart from wishing it wasn't here and this.

'Wasn't there, Joey. Wasn't there, mate.'

'No,' says Joe, his tone unmistakably suggesting that his friend wasn't the type who would be. 'Don coffeed me up and kept me away from getting banged up and losing my fucking job. Don's a good guy.'

'Fuck,' says the tall boy, for no apparent reason, kicking a chair and quickly regretting it.

28

'Stop that, Mozzer, stop that now. Sit the fuck down.'

Before we get Mozzer settled, I manage to move them to one of the alcoves at the back of the café, where Mozzer can stretch out on the bench along the back wall and be invisible from the street. The recumbent Mozzer looks like a stretched out orang utang. The blond also sits with his back supported; he's still gulping and unable to look anyone else in the eye.

'Stag night,' says Joe, seeing the question in my face. 'First, the guy it was for got fed up – he doesn't usually drink much - and went home. Then we lost the rest of them. Mozzer's already made a twat of himself mooning at people and Mark's been sick twice. If I take them out again, we'll finish up nicked and that's going to be my job on the line again –'

'You don't believe in a quiet life, do you, Joe?'

'Oh, for fuck's sake....yeah, O.K., Don, whatever. Fetch us coffee, please nicely, before me and these two fucking idiots go down –'

'Coffee be fucked. Bring us a beer, you old bastard.'

Joe is on his feet and my assessment of his combative ability is accurate enough, because Mozzer, who's at least three inches taller, turns his face to the wall.

'Shut the fuck up, Mozzer!' Joe shouts. 'If it wasn't for me, you'd already be banged up, you tosser, flashing your arse and screaming at blue lights! Just shut it and do what you're told!'

Mozzer flounces and sulks, like the kid he still is.

'O.K., Joe,' I say, as Blondie starts swaying again. 'Black coffee coming up, though if Blondie here throws up on my floor, he's going to clean it up.'

'Sure, Don, sure.'

I take a look into the back room. Maggie is dozing, slouched sideways in the armchair, the brandy half

29

finished beside her. I remember the pills in my pocket. Maybe, just a few would be ideal nightcaps for wild boys. Three dropped into a sizable coffee pot and they'll never notice the difference; that should do the trick.

Twenty five past four, and the guys are sleeping peacefully in the alcove as Maggie and I emerge to take a look.

'Oh, Don, how sweet,' Maggie says. Her doze and her brandy have brought her eyes back and managed to partly resurrect the real Maggie, the survivor, the tough old girl who bashes on regardless.

'Sweet wouldn't be my word, Maggie. And I wouldn't get too close, if I was you.'

But, of course, she does; I suppose working in hospitals and pubs has made her immune. She kisses Joe softly on the cheek.

'Sleeping beauty, eh,' she says. 'It's strange, isn't it, Don, how frightening things can be kind of cut out, just like that?'

'Do they frighten you, these boys?'

'Oh, sometimes. Almost everything does now, Don, sometimes, though I rely a lot on the invisibility of old ladies. If they see you at all, they sort of look through you. But you know what they could do to you if they had a mind to. And now I know what I could do to me if I have a mind to. It's about what might be and what is. The older you get, the harder it is to see the difference. And the more frightening the might be gets.'

'Well, just now, Maggie, the might be's a bunch of sleeping kids.'

'Yes, Don. It is, isn't it?'

She comes over to me and kisses me lightly on the cheek.

'Thanks for the drinks, Don; I'll settle up with you next time around. I'd going to carry on my snooze at home. I'm feeling more like it now. Have you got the rest of those pills?'

I look at her carefully, and she knows exactly why.

'No, that was a one-off. People have them, don't they? When someone's there for them, like you've been for me, it passes, and it's passed for me. This time, the might be was you, darling. And I know now another use for the pills. Nightcaps for wild boys. It's a good trick, is that, Don.'

'You know where we are, Maggie. It won't always be me, but you're one of our favourite customers - we'll always look after you.'

I put the pills in her hand and kiss her cheek. 'Go well, Maggie. Keep in touch.'

Dawn is well on as I wave her away, the morning light guiding her home.

A NORMAL LIFE

John even had some control of the darkness now. Not long after he'd found his garage, his blankets (left outside a charity shop early one morning) and his tiny calor gas stove which he'd just walked out of a camping equipment shop with, he'd discovered a working torch near the rail tunnel where, precariously, he used to sleep. That tunnel had been dangerous and very frightening; if trains had ever passed through it, it must have been long ago, but water and other moisture dripped from its roof, rats the size of cats seemed to be scurrying round, and people sometimes came into it to do hidden things to or with each other.

The garage was a lucky break. There was a disused factory on the edge of town, most of it so firmly boarded up that access was impossible, but four garages stood on the perimeter next to a patch of concrete. John watched them for a while and nearly abandoned the whole idea when a pick-up drew up and a hefty, cloth capped man opened one of the garages and unloaded a number of oddly shaped objects John couldn't make out. But the tunnel and other semi-exposed spots were the only choices; he needed something warmer and more secure. He approached cautiously and found, to his delight, that one of the other garages, though not open, had enough of a tiny gap between the doors for him to force it.

An indescribably bad smell, but it was not death bad, which John, for some reason, knew he knew; no-one could have been in it for a long time. The place was scattered with indiscriminate junk, but some of it was quite useful junk; the brackets on the inside of the doors were obviously there for securing planks to be put across to lock the doors and the lock itself just needed some adjusting to the woodwork around it. John's triumph was complete when he found a key, presumably the spare, on a high shelf near the door.

He worked quickly and efficiently, despite the rot gut stuff still living in him from the day before; not for the first time, his mind irritatingly occupied itself with vague questions while he was trying to concentrate entirely on what he was doing. He was at least, now, showing himself to be resourceful and taking advantage of what luck came his way; how come he still could not place, with any sense of sureness and reality, exactly who he was and why this strange life had claimed him? Why was he so convinced he could not go back to the life he'd lived before, when he couldn't remember with any clarity or confidence what that life was?' Why was he so positive that he had cut himself off for ever, when he had no clear memory of where or why? Why could he not even tell himself with absolute certainty that his name was John? A couple of men had called him it and he had responded to it, but with that feeling, common now to everything in his life, of chronic doubt.

But what, after all, did it matter – only now mattered, food and shelter, survival some kind of safety. In just three hours, he had the doors firmly shut and locked. Of course, the only light as yet came through narrow gaps above and beside the doors, but for the first time in what seemed like an age of cold and misery, John was not only sheltered from the weather but, even more importantly as he'd come to realise, people. He wasn't naive enough to believe that most locks could protect a determined break in by someone who knew what they were doing, but the planks across the door would take a lot of busting off and why would anyone want to make the effort?

Finally, John felt himself safe enough to think. Sitting in the gloom, but the warmer, more protected gloom, the thoughts which normally just buzzed around in his mind like directionless flies, never remaining with him too long or developing further because of all the other demands, started gaining shape and direction.

First, foremost and obvious, what the hell was he doing in this state, living in filthy clothes, scavenging for bits of food and drink? He would struggle to define exactly what he meant by a normal life, but he did feel almost 100% certain that his present existence wasn't. Why didn't he go and see someone, give himself up to someone? I go through this over and over again, he thought, resting the back of his head against the wall. Even without being able to understand why, I cannot go back, there is a crime, or something desperate, terrible, unspeakable, involved in it, which forbids returning, which has sent me to this place like being sent to hell, to make the best of it I can. The old life disappeared for a reason which was unanswerable and conclusive, even if drink, terror and humiliation had dumbed his memory so much that he couldn't remember what it was. He had fallen a long way, down into a dirty pit; he needed to claw his way back. And that's what he was doing.

In the long, safe garage hours, snatches of memories began to come back, and, after the torch had been acquired, John took newspapers back with him to try to help the process.

Late Friday, the kids in bed, a couple of glasses of nice red, and Matt felt cheated. It should be unwind time, chilling into the weekend, but he knew well enough what the duties of the weekend would involve and he knew that the present relaxed and comfortable expression on Helen's face would soon be wiped off. The burden remained with them like monkeys on their backs, and no relief was on offer but these occasional insignificant interludes.

'Well,' she said, and her face had already changed, matching the weariness which insinuated itself into her voice like an ill-mannered gate crasher, 'how are we going to handle tomorrow? Nick and Amy are prepared to help you if need be; they're both still saying, bless them, that Uncle Peter comes first and anything else can wait or just be dropped.'

Matt put down his glass and made himself speak, though his voice sounded hoarse and congested.

'Yes, I know, that's what they're saying to us, but I heard them talking to each other during the week; they do that a lot, for brother and sister, and especially lately, which is probably a good thing. Nick's got an away match and doesn't yet know if he can play because he can't be sure how he'll get there, which is driving Mr. Dugdale the outspoken manager up the wall, especially as Nick doesn't feel able to explain his reasons for being unsure. Amy wants to shop in town because a couple of her friends have birthdays coming up and I don't trust those buses, quite honestly –'

His shoulders slumped and his midriff slackened. Helen placed one hand on his knee.

'They know you have to look for Peter, Matt. They're not really children any more. I can take care of one of them and we can think of something for the other. They would rather put up with such awkwardness as there is rather than know that you've given up.'

'Yes, I know. They're good kids.'

Matt sighed and his dark blue eyes misted over for a moment. Helen turned her face away; seeing him like

35

this sometimes seemed more than she could physically bear. All the boundless confidence and joy in life she associated with him, the tall, athletic young stranger who had crashed into her university life and occupied the entire horizon, seemed to be running slowly out of him, to be replaced by invasive little mounds of extraneous flesh, the jowls heavier, the middle wider.

The situation with his brother Peter was rushing him off in a direction where he had already started tentatively walking, the destination a frowsty, frustrated middle age, taking his life disappointments out on everyone, probably including his nearest and dearest. She, too, doubted herself more than she once had, and especially in her ability to stop the process happening in him.

'I'm not sure I can or should press on for much longer, Helen,' he said, still with the strange quiet voice-breaking hoarseness. 'I'm deeply sorry about what happened in Peter's life, more sorry than I can put into words, but ultimately, cliché as it is, our life has to go on '

'Yes, true.' She gazed back at him, her head tilted quizzically, the weird green eyes glistening at him in the way they did before one of her speeches, her Agincourt morale boosters, which he respected because he could see the concealed cost in the deathly pale of her complexion. She was going, he could see, to tell it again, and necessary as the telling probably was, a wild scream, in its infancy but growing rapidly, lived inside him; she could and would reinforce, reinforce, ad nauseam, and he was no longer sure of being able to match her toughness.

'Nick can travel with one of the other dads; several of them always take their cars. Amy can take a bus like lots of other people do or even, for God's sake, walk; it's only just over a mile. Their lives will be mildly inconvenienced at worst. Your brother's life has been torn apart. We have to remind ourselves why, Matt, we have to keep doing that, or his life will just be shunted up a siding somewhere and we will all have to suffer perpetually afterwards. A crash kills both his wife and his daughter, and even though that inquest stated quite specifically that the blame, between him and the oncoming driver, was at least 70/30 on the other guy, and even though the measurements proved he was nowhere near the limit, Carol's family decided he was responsible and treated him so badly at the funeral that we very nearly came to blows. Talk of prosecutions, revenge. Now he's gone. No-one seems to have the faintest idea where he's gone and even the police don't seem very interested; 'very sad, but big boy, forty three year old men really expected to look after themselves, resources just aren't there, to be honest. 'Over three weeks now and we still don't know where he is. I know how impossibly difficult it is for you, Matt, we all do and we're all feeling the pressure with you, and the time to give up will be your decision and we'll respect it. I just don't think we should until we have something like an answer, or are at least asking the right questions.'

She squeezed his arm. She had mostly been staring at the mantelpiece clock, as if obsessed with time while she ordered her thoughts, but now she looked at him again and saw that he was crying.

She was momentarily speechless and confused; crying men always had been more than she could deal with, especially when they were men like Matt.

He walked quietly away and shut the door behind him; she could hear him going in to the downstairs toilet. Helen looked at the glass he'd left as if hypnotised by it; she picked up her own and looked deeply into the dark redness, as if one simple colour could soothe the turmoil in her head.

Weekend nights and early mornings; they were the worst times to be in the open. He had seen what a group of drunken youths had done to a sleeping tramp in a city shop doorway early one Sunday morning and he'd run away blindly, staggering and weeping, any remaining pride squeezed out of him along with any realistic chance of helping the poor man when the thugs had finished with him. On his first Saturday in the locked garage, John was almost ecstatic with delight, contemptuously thrusting away the thought that such pleasure was excessive, a little crazy.

By now fixed up with matches and candles as well as his torch, he obtained – that all-purpose word - a few local and national newspapers and some discarded wine from supermarket scavenging. Terrified huddling in subways and stairwells, forbidding himself even the slightest noise or movement; insect ridden spots behind allotments, damp, smelly corners of woodland, well concealed floor spots in underground car parks, hotel back yards, corners of factories and depots, all remained exposed and all could be consigned to past ignorance. Tonight, he decided, after he'd had a glass or two and a check through the papers, the images and memories, voice snatches, vague pictures, associations registered but not explained, could be tackled with an eased, reflective mind which might at last make genuine progress.

But what actually happened was sleep, not far into the wine, a deeper, more satisfying sleep than he could remember for weeks, the dreams left buried for once, unspecified even if vaguely disturbing, like guns in the distance. He was half-conscious of murmuring, complaining voices surrounding him and heads nodding in his direction, when he realised, with shock enough to wake him in a second, that the voices were coming from

38

just outside the garage door; he could hear the words quite distinctly, even though he couldn't understand all of them. For a few minutes, they clashed angrily, competitively, with each other, then one, stronger and more distinctive, continued alone.

'You know the fucking rules, you Stoneham punk.' Stoneham was a district on the other side of the city, which John had drifted into one night and drifted rapidly out of again.

'You're bang out of fucking order being here. This is our land. You know the rules.'

A great crash against the door and John shrunk away against the wall, urgently needing to piss. Then a sound impossible to understand, following by a long, sighing groan and another, lesser crash as a figure fell against the bottom of the door. A succession of clumps and breaths, some sounding of effort, enjoyment or both, some half gasps, half groans of real pain. Then the easier noises faded away and there were only clumps in endless sickening succession. Eventually, nothing but faint, animal like shuffling and sobbing.

John could not control himself anymore and got very carefully to his feet to go and piss in the corner, with vague, dismissive thoughts about airing the place. He sat down again and faced an annoyance turning itself slowly inwards.

He knew what he'd just heard and had a good idea of what he was hearing now. But other truths, other realities, the tattered remnants of what must once have been a normal life, he had been able to simply put aside as things which fitted into normal lives but not this one, like the fact that stealing was a crime, that breaking into other people's property, even if unused, was a crime. For some reason he couldn't understand, this situation, none of his business at any point, he couldn't so easily dismiss, and his failure irritated him.

To open that door was mega-dangerous; even if only the attacked boy was left, to rely on the rest of them having completely gone was an enormous gamble. All he needed to do was sit quietly, showing no light, and wait for the problem to go away, either for the boy to scramble away if he was able to or for an ambulance to take him if he wasn't.

Minutes passed, and John tried to close his eyes to the wounded boy outside the door and sounds which might well be about slow death, long low groans, occasional childish, snuffling sobs, swearing and sometimes animal-like grunts of real pain. He rested his head against the wall again and felt an inexplicable but overpowering sense of death everywhere around him, recent, fresh and raw, so overwhelming that he could do nothing but bow his head to it, say prayers which he didn't fully understand and accept meekly its victimisation of him.

Then a huge, totally unexpected jolt of pride and shame galvanised him into a spasm of action like a long strike of lightning and at the end of it, he'd opened the garage door and, without looking out or around, dragged the prone figure into the garage, locked the door and put the planks back in place.

John sat down against the wall again, winded and gasping as if he'd run a race, and took several deep breaths. The boy's breathing was still audible; he was murmuring, panting unevenly and now giving out little more than occasional child-like quavering sobs. John moved him gently further from the door and shifted his back up against the wall. A white boy, well-built, broad-shouldered, certainly no more than seventeen, smooth-skinned, his almost alabaster paleness streaked with

40

tears, dirt and snot. John edged his leather jacket away and recoiled from the state of the shirt beneath, already a spreading bloody mess and with blood still trickling between the boy's thin, shaking fingers. John pulled back the cloth of the shirt and saw the extent of the wound, a good two inches wide, spreading and gaping, while all the time the boy's eyes rested on him with a desperate childish trust.

'A mobile.' John spoke for the first time. 'You must have a mobile; all you kids have mobiles, where is it? They didn't do all this to you just to pinch your bloody mobile.'

John noted with detached interest, spectating on his own life, that he instinctively knew both of these asserted facts without understanding why.

'Gonna die. Gonna die. They stuck me like a pig. They battered me.'

'Mobile,' John insisted. 'Where?'

The boy's eyes narrowed and his head rose a little, as if the idea of rescue had only just occurred to him. He nodded down to the lower left pocket of the jacket. John seized it and instantly realised, with another shock like a wakening, that he knew exactly what to do with these things, and he'd picked it up and called 999 before stopping to think about it.

Then, from outside the door, people noises returned.

'God,' said the leading voice again. 'Where the fuck is he? Where THE FUCK is he?'

Matt stopped the car and turned off the engine. He was exhausted, defeated and deeply unhappy. From any sane point of view, this was the end, and he would have to go home and confess to them all, his wife and his children, that he had failed completely. They would be sympathetic. He may even have a few more of Helen's

41

Agincourt speeches to deal with and he would have to just shake his head sadly at her, the man who could do nothing, the man whose inadequacy was now all too sadly apparent. He suspected the relationship would never be the same again.

He'd been everywhere both probable and feasible; he had moved on to long-shot possibilities and scarcely imaginables. Now, he knew, he was moving into high-risk territory and the only rational course of action was to withdraw, keep in touch with the police and put out what soundings he could. But the last defeated trek home stuck unpalatably in his gullet.

This place, a long disused factory, was notoriously dangerous to explore and reputably infested with the lowest kinds of criminality, especially in the dark; he would be putting himself in immediate danger of accident, injury or assault which would be difficult to justify either to the police or his own family. Yet the debate went on inside him; he had been taking risks for days, rooting out the homeless, almost invariably men or boys, in situations where they could certainly have combined to damage him had they chosen to do so, and now and then they'd seemed to be not far away from it, resenting his questions, even his presence. He was not by nature a courageous or foolhardy man, and the effort of summoning up what resources he could, again and again, took a heavy accumulative toll. In the distance, near a small block of four garages, Matt heard sounds and then saw movements; he got out of his car and walked towards what looked like a group of boys outside one of the garage doors. About two hundred yards away, he realised, with a lurch of his heart and a sudden awareness of the tiredness in his limbs, that something violent was going on there. One of them noticed him and turned, and his body language, shoulders thrown back, head jutted forward, spoke resentment and aggression.

'Please, I'm looking for – ' Matt started to say.

'This is private land, and private business. Get the fuck out of our face, man.'

Something glinted suddenly in the darkness and Matt realised with a shiver of cold through his guts that it was the blade of a knife. The boy who had spoken shifted slightly to his right and Matt saw a prone figure just behind the group of them. They all began to move towards him. Matt's remaining courage and spirit marched blindly away; he turned and ran for his car with all his remaining strength, hearing their footsteps gaining behind him. He'd only just started the car when the leading one of them was clattering against his boot; he drove frantically away, noticing all four of them standing in the same spot, shouting and gesticulating, for as long as he remained in sight.

At the end of his own quiet, slumbering road, Matt stopped the car, let his head fall and gasped for air. He raced across the road and vomited over a fence into the neighbourhood park. Then he returned to his car and breathed in slowly and deliberately until he'd convinced himself he was empty and calm enough to face the defeated return to the house.

John listened with little sympathy to the conversation happening just outside the door. Bewildered and confused, they sounded much like the frightened children they essentially were, still wrapped up in elaborate games which their pride demanded had real adult actions introduced into them. John had made police and ambulance calls and been as explicit about the place as he could; the police in particular, he thought, would know this spot well enough. He'd ripped apart one

43

of his three stolen shirts to wrap strips round the boy's wound to at least stem the blood loss. The boy was even paler and close to unconsciousness from a combination of shock and loss of blood.

John had realised, a propos of nothing, that his name was actually Peter, though how and why he suddenly knew this, he couldn't understand. The idea that someone would come and attend to this boy and leave him alone to continue life in his garage had also become mysteriously absurd; there was an ending in this somewhere. Awareness grew within him of recent, long and painful dealings with both police and ambulances, dangerous and devastating, though he still couldn't place exactly what the events and circumstances amounted to.

'That geezer, him we chased,' said one of the voices outside. 'He's told someone, someone's fetched the Stoneham bastard away.'

'We only saw him ten minutes ago, Craig, you fucking idiot, what's he got, a fucking space beam?' Two of them laughed, deep-voiced, nervously, and then the lead voice silenced all the others again.

'He's got in there.' A bang against the door. 'I dunno how, but he's got in there. Or someone's fetched him in there.'

Peter closed his eyes and dropped his head. As the volume of banging grew on the door and fingers tried to squeeze into the tiny gaps of light, Peter could see that the boy before him was unconscious, the shirt bandage soaked. Memories now started to march into his mind unchecked, and he wondered at the great torrent of cruelty which seemed to have been irrationally, inexplicably, unleashed on him in the recent past. He turned, puzzled, at yells of triumph from outside the door, and then saw that they had succeeded in setting fire

44

to the door base. Little flames were beginning to lap around the corner.

Peter looked from the boy to his wrists; he felt sure that the boy would also have a knife on him somewhere, and that could at least give him a chance of a last fight. He was debating whether he had enough time to search the boy when, first faintly and then in a cacophony of noise spreading all over the night, sirens sounded, the boys ran away, and he opened the garage door to a great yellow and blue extravaganza of light as if he'd suddenly stepped out to an audience.

Matt was reliving every moment of his flight, except that this time, the boys had caught up with him and two of them were holding him down on the back seat while another, smiling to himself, seemed to be preparing, relishing, an approaching moment of pure sadism for his own perverse pleasure. The ringing phone sounded into the darkness like rescue arriving, and he sprang up in the bed with a yell of triumph and relief.

'Matt? What the hell –'

Helen looked and noted how the long, slumping back raised and stiffened, very slowly, from all the way down at the waist to the rising and spreading shoulders, as the phone conversation went on. She felt a growing pleasure herself, an instinct speaking the end of a long bad stretch. All he was saying was 'Right' or 'Yes' or 'Great,' and eventually, 'I'm coming now; I'll be there in fifteen minutes.'

Helen glanced at her watch; it was just short of twenty past five. When she looked back to him, he was already dressing, talking over his shoulder and from his back as he moved about the room.

'It's Peter. At least, it looks hellishly like it. That was Staff Nurse Reynolds, Beth Reynolds, in Accident and

Emergency, the senior nurse on the night of the crash. She's good with names and faces, she says, but she'd have to have been pretty bad not to have recognised Peter Foster, after the two days he went through in there and the kind of treatment he got from his wife's family. They've brought in some kid who's been stabbed and Peter came with him; he wasn't going to, but the kid insisted. The kid says Peter saved his life. He's on a drip, this kid, but he's survived. Peter, she says, looks wasted, unshaved, older, filthy and only vaguely aware of who he is. She says she got him to agree that she could phone his brother to prove to him who he is. She says it is Peter, it is absolutely Peter, beyond any shadow of a doubt whatsoever, whatever the dirt, blood, confusion.'

Matt sat on the edge of the bed to put his shoes on and she heard quiet, uneven breathing, like a child anticipating a treat, involuntary and beyond his present control. She put one hand on the place where his shoulder and neck joined and felt the hard, unyielding tension of his skin.

'Go bring him back, love. There'll be lots of time for rest now.'

He turned and kissed her, the way he did it when he meant it, which was most of the time.

Peter had been standing, awkwardly, in a corridor, bemused and disorientated, but entirely himself, when Beth Reynolds insisted he move into her own office. After another great effort of memory, he recognised her, and everything which had happened in this place marched back, though this time there was a distance, a detachment, which hadn't been there before. At the time when it was actually happening, he had no defences, no way of making his way through it and nothing very much, he could now see with greater balance, being offered from

46

people who he might reasonably have expected to be supportive. Only Matt had stood by him at the time, and now there was enough space for him to be able to generate a little resentment in himself. And, of course, other major differences this time – the clear sympathy, even respect, of the police, the generous response of the boy's family, albeit with a few curious and anxious looks directed at his physical state and appearance, and even the paramedics joining in the general chorus of approval.

He sat just in front of Nurse Reynolds' desk, grateful for her consideration; he'd been aware in the corridor of the looks being directed at him and he now needed very much to clean up.Losing Kate, such a wife, and Jen, such a daughter, was still so great a cataclysm that what kind of future there might be daunted him at the thought of its painful construction, but that plunge, that sudden lurch into total amnesia and the loss of any knowledge of even where he'd used to live, seemed somehow as much extreme suffering as he was now prepared to permit. Whatever price had needed paying, he'd paid it; something else needed to happen.

He looked up and saw Matt standing in the doorway. A long, uninhibited release of a bear hug, while Beth looked round from the ward doors and lost even the half per cent doubt of it.

'You need a wash, kid,' Matt said quietly. 'Let's go home.'

SAVING GRACE

I am on posh territory, an international conference centre, no less, looking at my gorgeous best. Made to measure light grey suit, with some company's badge on my lapel in case of officious sniffing about. I have several such badges, provided by clients who want to make sure I will be on the premises when they need me to be. All of them are temporarily well away from wives, girlfriends, boyfriends etc., and staying in anonymous hotels where an hour or two of hanky-panky the way they like it relieves the conference tedium.

I use Peter for work purposes, that's Peter, not Pete. I don't lay bricks with my cleavage on view. Peter it is.

On this particular occasion, I notice a guy, mid-thirties, quite nicely put together, hard eyes, bullish neck, probably heading for fat fifties, watching me carefully from a sofa about twenty yards away. Not one of my regulars. And those eyes, might well be SM. I'm not in the mood. Anyway, I don't have to work that hard any more. I'm a high-class hooker, not your park bog anyone's for a fiver.

He's now on an armchair only seven or eight yards away, and the steady look is unnerving me. He looks like he wants to fuck me or murder me, and not necessarily in that order.

Still, like I said, I'm not desperate these days, so giving him a bit of sass might settle matters quickly. I've got work to do.

'I don't know what you're staring at. In that suit, I doubt you could afford me.'

A sort of smile, and a slight nod of the head, as if I've just done something he expected me to do. A homicidal maniac with ESP. Terrific.

'George, isn't it? Mr. George Edwards?'

He knows my name. My real name. I'm spooked enough to keep schtum. We sit staring at each other, like a game of chicken.

'My guvnor wants to talk to you.'

'Your guvnor? What are you, a state?'

'Detective Chief Inspector Michael Payne. He's my guvnor. He wants to talk to you.'

I tut like only I can.

'Does he now? I might have known. I'm breaking no law sitting here, nor am I under any obligation to talk to anyone. Sod off and find a pickpocket. The place is crawling with them.'

Oddly enough, the eyes sort of relax a little, like a kind of 'come off it, will you'?

'George, I'm not allowed to tell you publicly what this is about. But I can tell you it's about someone you know. Someone you know very well. And you won't have to go to a station; we have a temporary office here when the big conferences are on.'

He stands up, and waves one arm in the direction he wants me to go. Maybe he used to be a traffic cop. What the hell, I think. A high-ranking plod could be very useful. I could be his part-time private dick.

And soon here I am, in the big man's office, and quite plush, as offices go. State of the art computers, even a vase of flowers or two. We can have a civilised conversation about home furnishings before he bangs me up.

And here is the man himself, taller than his bag man, and with quite intelligent eyes for a plod. His first words also sound different from the customary Ploddish. Conversational, almost friendly. Maybe he's looking for a freebie after all. Handcuffs and truncheon job.

'I am going to call you George for the moment - George. For you, this is a mix of the professional and the personal, and we're off the record for the time being.'

'Don't give me that,' I say, but I do sit down where indicated, a nice armchair even. 'There's no off the record with you lot. You're either recording it up front or recording it down below. I haven't flown here on my own carpet'

'You have a sister, don't you, George?'

Right where it hurts, that one. I sort of metaphorically close my legs, in case they've decided to play really dirty.

'Do I? Why is that of interest to you? If you're the incest police, I deny it all. It may have escaped your notice, but I'm not what you'd call a ladies' man –'

He stands up with elaborate patience. He nods at the bagman, and now it seems there are just the two of us. And a whole world of memories is starting to crash over me.

'You have a sister, two years older than yourself, whose name is Grace. You left home not long after she left home. Violent, abusive parents. More specifically, father, your mother being unable to stop him. She even watched sometimes though, didn't she? You tried to stop Grace from going, didn't you, for your sake as well as hers?'

It still comes again, wherever I am, whatever I'm doing. Those last few minutes, my single ally in the world deserting the sinking ship.

50

She could move very quietly, could Grace. She'd had to learn. But we had an instinct, we always knew exactly where the other was. The quietest of taps in the hall outside my door; I think she slightly bumped her bag against the skirting board.

I get out of bed and open my door. Very quietly, I've learned that lesson as well. She's stood there, fully dressed, with that bag she uses when Dad orders another shop.

I just mouth a question. She signals me to follow her downstairs, and three yards away from the front door, we have our last conversation.

'I'm going, Georgie,' she whispers. 'I can't bear it any more. I can't get over thinking about the things he's done to me. And the things he's done to you.'

'Yes. Or he did. I'm sixteen, I'm too big for him. He's started being a bit scared of me.'

'There's a word for it, George. It's abuse. Physical and sexual abuse.'

'I know. I'll go when I'm ready. But I'll pay him out first.'

'Pay him out? How...?' Her eyes are as wide as they go, and they're big eyes, sort of grey like Mum's, but without Mum's weariness and defeat.

'I don't know. I'm still working it out. Go back to bed, Grace, please. We can talk about it, work something out.'

A rumble from upstairs, and we both jump. But it's just Dad snoring. Seven pints, I reckon, by the sound of it. Snores and retches would mean he threw in a brandy or two.

She moves a bit closer to the front door. For a moment, I think she's just going to charge through it. But she stops, with her hand on the door handle.

'Josie Rushton wrote away to this ad for working as a nanny in London, bed and board included. They accepted her, so then I wrote as well and now they've accepted me. Better than sweating away in a shop. Better than putting up with him. I'm eighteen, I can do what I like. I'll write to you, Georgie. Take care.'

Two light clicks, one to open the door, one to shut it. And that's it. I'm standing on the doormat in my pants, sniffing and snuffling, with my only ally in this place gone. And not well gone, either. I know Josie Rushton. Nice kid, but incredibly naïve and a bit simple. A nanny, eighteen years old, with no training in looking after children? It stinks to me.

Another snoring crescendo upstairs. 'Choke, you old bastard. Do us all a favour. Don't expect an ambulance.'

My own muttered words in a strange, breathless tone. I could be dreaming. But I'm not.

'Yes, Chief Inspector, mega-plod, whatever I'm supposed to call you. Yes, of course I tried to stop her. I had two shit parents and a nice sister. She's off, I'm left with two shit parents, one out of his mind most of the time and the other like a mobile dishrag. So, sob, sob. What's it to you?'

He says nothing for a minute, just sits there looking at me, curiously, like he's summing me up, though not sexually. It's not what I'm used to. Guys who don't fancy me rarely have any other interest.

'You're an aggressive so and so, George, aren't you? We know quite a lot about you now. Your work with a so-called escort agency; none of the regular pimps for you, eh? You sorted one of them out too, didn't you? When did you get so physical, George? Kicking seven bells out of Daddy, was it?'

He's under the skin again. He ought to be a policeman, this guy. Oh, yes, he is, isn't he?

'So what? You're pulling me in for that? Not many juries would do more than a suspended sentence, Mr. Chief Inspector. Between the ages of seven and fifteen, that old bastard did just about everything you could imagine to me, and some you might not be able to. They'd acquit me just to stop me telling them the details.'

'And Grace, I suppose?'

My eyes are suddenly wet, and it maddens me.

'Yes, and Grace as well. What's it to you?'

'We know where she is, George. We know exactly where she is.'

I'm on my feet. This is what I came to London for.

I got everything organised. I went round to the Rushtons, during the day when the old man would be out. I wormed the details out of old Doreen, almost as naïve as her daughter.

'She's on her way now, George, that's for sure. London; rich people's kids.'

Should I tell her what I'm afraid of? Maybe not. Maybe, even, I'm wrong. But that's why it needs checking out.

I picked my moment with the old man. He'd chased Mum out to get him some beer or something. He told me to sod off upstairs and leave him alone; I worry him now, I really do. I'd got hold of a baseball bat; you can get hold of anything if you know where to go. And how to oblige people.

He was sat in his chair, glass on his table, reading his paper. I came in, so quiet, like a fucking human mouse, scurrying up behind him. He got the bat three times, and then he was on the floor, and I had a field day. I kicked him and he shouted, then he cried, then he went quiet. Then I picked up my stuff and left.

Train to London, I had a bit of money from part-time this and that. Cruising the bus stations and stuff. I was going to find Grace and bring her home. Or help her set up in London.

Then I'm standing outside the address old Doreen gave me. It doesn't look the kind of house people who employ nannies would live in. People who employ dealers, pimps, hookers, maybe. Nannies, no.

I knocked on the door, and my heart was going like a train. A big guy appeared, in a bad suit, with a lot of dark stubble and a lip looking permanently fixed in a sneer.

'Hi. Do you recognise this girl, please?'

He looks at it for about half a second.

'No,' he says, and I know that's all I'm going to get.

'She's supposed to have come here to work –'

He sort of grimaces, and moves back into the house.

'Fuck off, son, there's a good boy.'

Banged door. I hung around, trying to peer in. Two of them came out, oinking like pigs in heat. I left.

That was the last I heard from Grace, until standing here in front of Detective Chief Inspector Payne – he introduced himself to me, with a 'by the way' attached to it. He's confusing me, because he's being vaguely nice to me, which isn't my customary experience with policemen. 'Move along, puffta, before I nick you for soliciting,' is more their style, and that's the gentle ones. My guts are in my boots. What's he getting at? Is he going to be asking me to identify a body, or what? Jesus, not Grace, please God, not Grace.

'You came to London looking for Grace, and when you'd followed up what leads you could, which wasn't very many, it occurred to you that you had nowhere to live. And the police might be looking for you –'

'Well, GBH with a baseball bat and a stout pair of boots. They're not going to pat me on the head and give me a lolly, are they?'

'He said he'd had a fall, George. When he was drunk. Right down the stairs.'

Now I am standing gaping at him and he is looking fixedly at me, as if he expects me to burst into song or something

'You're joking me. What would he say that for?'

'I don't know, George. Maybe he wanted to be sure you'd gone, and you wouldn't come back and do him again. And he got over it. Your mother is perhaps not as useless as you might think. She had an ambulance to him in time. You have no case to answer, George.'

I needed to sit down.

'So what the fuck am I doing here?'

'You're here because we know where Grace is.'

I eyed him carefully. He was becoming more visible, was Detective Chief Inspector Michael Payne. But I'm feeling something. I don't mean fancying him – the day I start having daydreams about Romance in Plodland will be the day I book myself into the funny farm. But, stupid as it seems, since he is Mega Plod and I am rent – high class rent, definitely, but rent all the same – there is something about him that says he's sort of been to the places I've been, before being a policeman.

I should never have given up on Grace. Yes, it's true, she never contacted me, but that's probably because she couldn't. I got so taken up with the freedom of having my own money, my own place to live, scruffy little flat as it is, even if I did have to do all sorts of stuff with men I usually felt nothing for. Grace just got lost off. No more.

'I'm listening,' I said quietly. 'Sir.'

Grace was one of those kids who was always laughing. Even after the old pig started doing what he

55

did, she would still be laughing when we went out to the market or somewhere. We always had to stop near the infants' school so she could watch the little kids; she was crazy about having a kid of her own. And I could do stuff which made her laugh, stupid dances, animal noises. I loved to hear her laugh.

DCI Payne laid on it on the line. Where the house was, how many guys were in there, how many girls were 'on offer' – it made my stomach turn.

'It's supposed to be a B and B, but if you go in there asking for 'special services,' they will probably fix you up with one of the girls in the cellar. It's one of these Victorian places with a huge cellar, which is where they keep the girls. Well-equipped basement rooms.'

Too much, even for a street guy. I had a wet face.

'Gracie,' I muttered. 'She didn't deserve that.'

'No,' he said, and his voice was different. 'But your Grace is a bright girl, George.'

'Oh, yes, she is that.' A memory suddenly returned, and even made me laugh. 'She got hold of some sleeping tablets, probably from my mother, who used them like sweeties. When he came back from the pub and went up to her room, she'd pour him a beer and put two tablets in it. Never failed. And when he woke up, he couldn't remember a thing.'

'Yes, that's Grace. She might have been naïve about the nanny training thing, but she's come on since then. She's managed to get hold of a phone the guys in there don't know about. Probably offered some guy extras to get her it.'

My head dropped. I knew about 'extras.'

Payne carried on regardless.

'She's got a whole collection of stuff on it, enough to send every guy in there down for years; pictures, sound, even photoed documents, girls' stolen passports. She's

56

managed to hide it from them so far, and she's even made contact with us.'

'Well, why the fuck don't you go in and get her out?'

He sighed. 'George, my old son, you've lived on the streets long enough to know things are never simple. She doesn't want to be in there when the place is raided; she's afraid all her evidence will get lost in the scuffle. These guys are violent beings, and they'll do anything to avoid being nicked. She wants to get out and give us her evidence before the raid. She's discovered a hatch, probably the bottom of what used to be the coal chute, which will open if forced. But she won't leave the other girls until she knows the raid is coming, and she knows getting out is a two person job.'

'Well, send a guy in to get her out.'

'There isn't a man in the world she trusts, George, in or out of uniform. Except one.'

His eyes rest on me, and I'm puzzled for a moment; it's something like sympathy. Then, of course, the penny drops. I'm not as quick as Grace, but I get there eventually.

'You mean me?'

He nodded. 'You know what she told us? 'No girl could have a better brother than George. He even took the old man into his own room sometimes, to save him coming into mine. The old man could hardly tell the difference....'"

Which did it. My street cool flew right out of the window. For about ten seconds, I blubbed like a baby.

Payne didn't look disgusted, or embarrassed, or pitying. He gazed down at the desk, waiting for me to finish.

'Meaning Grace was telling us to find you, George. So we did. It wasn't too difficult.'

Such an undramatic, laid-back policeman; where he came from wasn't so different from where we came from, I'd guess. I know a lot about guys, a hell of a lot. I know my fellow men like I know the back of my hand, and every other part of my anatomy, for that matter.

'You've been somewhere with this, haven't you, Mr. Payne?' I said.

He looked at me, thinking things over.

'I grew up in care, George. Being everything everyone else wanted me to be, until I decided to be what I wanted to be. It'll come to you, believe me.'

So this time, with me and the Force, it wasn't being warned, strip searched, remanded or interrogated, it was off to a dim South London street of Victorian villas. With a plan.

We parked a few streets away, Payne and me in the front, the guy who'd come up to me in the conference centre and a young PC in the back. No-one would get curious about a car with four guys inside it. It wasn't the kind of neighbourhood where curiosity was advisable.

For about the hundredth time, DCI Payne went over it.

'Grace will trigger it with a ten-minute signal; if it takes even five minutes longer than that, we're going in anyway. We had to make a few conditions too. When you get out, run to the first car; the back seat will be empty –'

'Yes, I've got it, Mr. Payne,' I said, just a little wearily. 'I get in and out of complicated places all the time. It's what I do. My clients often don't reside in the most upmarket postcodes.'

Something like a grin crossed his face, and was immediately wiped away like a notice board, like grins weren't allowed on duty.

Yes, I've blagged and bluffed my way in and out of a variety of places, and I told myself this was just another one, but the physical signs were there; a bit of breathlessness, an increased heart rate. This wasn't just my work, this was about Grace. I did what I always do, noting carefully the geography of the place as I went into it.

At the end of a short corridor there was something which I suppose passed as a reception desk, where a sour-faced middle-aged lady watched me approach her.

'Mr. Smithson,' I said. 'I phoned earlier.'

'O.K., love,' she said, and cracked what she probably thought was a welcoming smile, but seemed more like a Cheshire cat in its death throes.

'Special services, if that's O.K.. Do I book in advance? Gemma?'

'You know Gemma? You been here before?'

'I know of Gemma by personal recommendation. And I think I can tell you, Ma'am, that she won't be disappointed, you know what I mean?'

'Well, you're the saucy sod, aren't you? We'll phone your room when it's time.'

I found myself up one flight of stairs in Room 2, which looked like most low grade B and B rooms look. Functional would be flattering, but it did at least have a shower. I put my bag down. The camera was pathetically obvious, supposedly disguised as a light fitting. Anything they thought out of the ordinary, I'd be out on my arse. As I went to close the door, I saw a huge man eyeing me from the reception area. I would have been more intimidated if he hadn't been wheezing like an asthmatic bear. I smiled and winked; he just stared.

I waited for an eternity, and just being normal strained my patience. I had a beer, read a paper someone had left lying around. I had a shower and strolled around nude, just to convince them I hadn't tumbled to the camera. And give old prune face a treat.

59

At seven o'clock, someone knocked on my door. It was the big bear man, breathing heavily and looking hard, or doing his best to.

'It's your time,' he said breathily, like a kind of fat Grim fucking Reaper.

Down to the basement, he knocks softly on a fancy red door, then opens it without waiting for an answer.

'Two hours max, as agreed,' he said. I don't remember agreeing to it, but I wasn't going to be around for two hours anyway.

She was sitting on the bed. I could see it was Grace, by the way she sat, the profile of her, the angle of her head.

She turned her face to me. I was afraid she would shriek or something. I closed the door behind me. She gave me a full eyes and mouth wide open silent gape and ushered me in, nodding at the camera, which was concentrated largely on the bed area, and we moved out of its range to the little recess which passed as her kitchen. The place was a dungeon; reasonably well-appointed as dungeons go, but a dungeon all the same.

We'd never been a very huggie-kissie pair of siblings, perhaps due to the squalor we grew up in, but we had a long bear-hug next to her sink, and then I whispered in her ear, 'can you tell when the camera's off?' She nodded, and went towards it for a closer look.

'It's off,' she said quietly, 'and it'll probably stay that way. You're not a celebrity visitor.'

'Bloody cheek,' I muttered.

We wasted no more time. We quietly left the room, not frontwards but backwards, left and further into the basement. There was no door that I could see and it was pitch dark. But she knew her way, and eventually, when we were no more than six inches away from it, I could just about make out a square door about two foot square.

'The old coal hole,' she whispered. 'I don't think they even know it's here.'

Most people wouldn't. But in places like this, back in the day, they tipped coal supplies off a truck down into the cellars of houses.

By the tiny light of her phone, she sent the alert signal to Payne. We had ten minutes.

There was one tiny handle on the top right hand corner of the chute door.

'You'll need to force it,' she said.

She wasn't kidding; I shoved, twisted and heaved. Suddenly, with a clang loud enough to wake the dead, it shot off its moorings altogether, revealing a dingy hole with thin blue light showing indistinctly.

Grace being Grace, she didn't hang about. She was up there like a rat up a pipe, and I made to follow her. Then I saw a big shape like a lurking gorilla in the dark.

'I knew you were bad news, you smart arse,' it just about managed to articulate, and then the plan seemed to be to pin me in a bear hug until help arrived.

Kick boxing is one of the pastimes it's useful to know something about if you follow a profession like mine, which has its unfortunate quota of violent, sadistic bastards. I made a quick calculation, like a snapshot of the shape of him, and went for his kneecap first; he had

a lot of weight riding on that. He sank down on one knee, enabling my other foot to connect with the side of his head. That ended his interest in the proceedings, but someone else was now clattering down the stairs.

As I squeezed my way up the coal hole, a face appeared below me and got my boot in it. Then I heard all hell breaking loose; the raid had started. Payne had timed it to the minute.

I emerged from the coal hole. It might have been some time since it saw coal, but it had acquired a few other substances and I was not at my freshest. Sure enough, the car was there as Payne had said it would be. Grace and me were a couple of scruff bags, but she didn't care and neither did I.

I was twenty two then and I'm twenty six now. I live in a comfortable flat in a nice part of town with my thirty year old civil partner Ian, and sometimes looking back just four years seems like visiting another world. I'm still a sassy, mouthy bastard and intending to remain so, perhaps indefinitely. But when I look back on supposedly rescuing Grace, I wonder who was rescuing who.

It didn't take me long to get off the game, which had a lot to do with the comments of guess who? Right enough – Grace. When you've seen your sister forced into that stuff, it kind of holds up a mirror to you. And of course, any woman who can react by taking out her persecutors as completely as Grace did has enough in her brain to point her little brother in the right direction.

I'd told her about a few of my punters, including Ian, who was a professional photographer, and one of the few I really liked – and fancied. She suggested I try and team up with him and get into journalism, starting by telling my own story – and, bless her, hers as well. I had my doubts, but I got in touch with the guy, and he seemed keen enough, so we put my tale together, using different names of course, with pictures of some places in town where I picked people up; I even checked it out with Mr. Payne, who liked the idea, as a warning to other young guys about the world they might be getting into. I talked about the vicious bastards, the good guys, the weird things some people wanted, usually toned down a bit. The paper lapped it up. And Ian and I became a team, both personal and professional, with the paper wanting us for our street cred. Soon other media got interested and the whole thing snowballed. I was suddenly the celebrity hooker, with my very own partner for the pictures. I thought it would just be a few months type of thing, but the paper started using the pair of us for other news stories, and now I'm on a wage with them.

As for Grace, she got herself involved with a women's organisation who track down people trafficked into the country by low-life bastards who want them to be hookers or slaves. She managed to track down Josie Rushton, who'd had a hard time of it, and the two of them live together now. I think they're lovers, but it's not my business. Ian and I like to go round there now and then; we have a good laugh with them. No agendas.

As for Plodland, I don't have many dealings with them these days. I'm almost a model citizen. We invited Mr. Payne to come to our partnership, partly as a laugh, I suppose, but he only and actually did, accompanied by Mrs. Payne, who looked a bit like what my mum might have looked like if she hadn't got caught up with the old bastard.

So who rescued who? I think sometimes Grace could have got out of there without me. She wanted me to do something good, like holding up a big unsubtle arrow in the face of a child saying 'this way to Goodland,' so that maybe I could believe that I was worth more than giving myself hook, line and sinker to every guy in the world who put his money on the table. That if I needed to give back to myself what the old man took away, such as pride, freedom, hope, self-esteem, this was the direction I should be moving in.

So maybe it was about saving Grace, but I think it was even more about my sister being my saving grace. Or at least making me see that I had one.

RAGE IN BLUE

Conroy shakes all six foot five of him out of bed at the sound of a front door click. He doesn't work by alarm clocks; his job isn't like that. But his restless being can only ever be in bed for so long, and something like a door click signifies that the day is up and running and that means he needs to be in it.

Naked but for a floral pair of boxers, one of his mostly closely-guarded secrets, he moves to the front door. One is a bill, one is unsolicited information about insurance, and one, a very slim envelope, contains a single sheet of paper. On it, a series of letters have been cut out from newspapers, and arranged to say:

'WE WILL SLIT YOUR THROAT AND WATCH YOU BLEED. YOU WILL HEAR FROM US.'

Ian Conroy has been recognised by his editor as the paper's number one investigative reporter; he is, or at least he gives the impression of being, thoroughly unspookable. But this paper causes him to look at it long and hard.

At first, he suspects that it is some kind of prank; he knows there are people in his media surroundings who are crazy enough to do something like this. Perhaps his Mr. Cool reputation, developed from his own reticence – using the word shyness for a huge man in his late twenties sounds bizarre - sometimes invites antagonistic gestures. But this is a bit much for a wind-up. If his editor Jack Pelham were to find out that one of his own staff were responsible, someone's guts might be had for Pelham's garters. Pelham is an ex-military man, with very specific ideas on what is and is not acceptable.

He dumps the piece of paper on the kitchen table and heads for the shower. Morning showers, in fact any time showers, are always useful for thinking things over, and he reflects on anyone he knows who might mean such a message seriously. A sleazy toe-rag called Silas, who uses a range of names and who is reputedly using a large house which is supposedly a hostel for rather less moral purposes, might be a candidate. His piece on Silas and his 'hostel' had contributed to the house being 'closed for repairs,' or more accurately shut down while Silas lies low, invents a new name or finds someone to front for him, then starts up again. But somehow, this doesn't have a Silas trademark. A violent assault on a journalist traced back to him or one of his guys might put him out of business permanently, and Silas, whatever else he is, is not stupid.

Then there was that man of the far right, Victor Syerson, posh voice, made to measure suits, incendiary website, who Conroy had named in his paper as an out and out fascist and a menace to the community, him and his 'Proud England' lot. Syerson's social media stuff was there for all to see, and however quickly they'd been removed following Conroy's investigation, many other people had seen them, including several lawyers Conroy happened to know.

As he moves back from bathroom to bedroom, Conroy thinks yes, it's the kind of thing Syerson could do; it gels with his theatrical turn of mind, with his sad attempts to make one large room and thirty-odd people look like a Nuremberg rally and his faked-up photos of 'immigrants' getting up to various outrages. He'd also been known to set his tame gorillas on to local media people who got too saucy. But Conroy's paper is big in the locality and Syerson could only remain in business by taking risks he had carefully calculated.

While getting through his coffee and toast, another likely candidate presents himself, one Harry Briggs, car salesman, whose nice new motors were quite likely to be crash write-offs or vehicles assembled from other vehicles which could well disintegrate at any time, regardless of where they were or who was in them. Conroy had gathered enough evidence to put together a detailed piece, the police had picked up on it, and Briggs' garage remained locked up and apparently deserted. However, getting round to prosecuting him seemed to be taking a long time, and Briggs was still at liberty. But Briggs has always struck him as very much all mouth and trousers, and probably wouldn't have the imagination for this, inventive as he could be when it came to cobbling old cars together.

Conroy has an appointment with his editor this morning anyway, a routine monthly catch-up, and he has few anxieties about his property; he lives in a modern block of generously-sized flats, with security cameras strategically dotted here and there, a terrace running along the front at his level and spectacular City views at the back. Anyone trying to break in would be visible from virtually the whole block.

Since he doesn't want Pelham to think that the piece of paper has particularly bothered him, he waits until all their routine business has finished before he puts the document on the table in front of Pelham.

'You've been in this business a lot longer than I have, Jack. Should I be worried?'

Pelham looks at the paper with distaste, his lip curled in contempt.

'If this is one of those juvenile fuckers in the news room, I will seriously kick their ass. Otherwise, I think it does need looking into. I was the one who made you the leading bother boy in the first place; huge guy, father a

66

Dublin cop, trained for the police, who else am I going to choose? Some kinds of shit are going to come with the territory. But I don't like my guys threatened, however amateurish the threat. It says you are going to hear from them; by phone, I'd reckon. Record it when it comes. Before it does, I'll mention this business to the police. I don't know how much good that will do, but I'll mention it anyway. In the meantime, son, be careful. Be bloody careful.'

Conroy heads home to do some phoning and research on his current stories. Only then does the niggling irritant at the back of his mind come into full shape.

'Anna,' he says aloud. Anna is due to visit him that evening, partly to talk about whether she should move in with him.

He curses quietly to himself. Anna, dark-eyed, enigmatic and beautiful Anna, the best thing that has happened to him in years, has finally acknowledged that she might seriously think about joining him in the flat, which was big for one person. She lives in a house share with three other people, two women and a gay man, and though the arrangement is convenient and economical, she wants more of her own space and privacy.

Anna is a primary school teacher, aged 25, who he visited when a local property scheme was threatening to lead to her school's demolition, meaning her pupils, mostly very local, would have to travel some distance to other schools. Most of the other schools had protested that they were not in a position to take such extra numbers. He saw it as a good story, and if it was to become a crusade, so be it.

What he didn't foresee, moody, taciturn Conroy, as most people seemed to regard him, was that Anna Shields didn't find him threatening because of his size and his few words, nor did she dismiss him as morally bankrupt because that's how she saw all journalists. Conroy, at twenty-eight, seems to have found someone who could see the whole of him. Only recently has it seriously occurred to him that he probably did need someone now, and that self-containment and self- reliance, solid professional qualities as they might be, could also represent routes to a dead end, some desolate place where his whole life, and not just half of it, could become so pointless as to be not worth continuing.

He gets home, banging his irritating piece of paper on the kitchen table, and spends the rest of his working day trying to concentrate on what he's doing at the same time as thinking through what he's going to say to Anna. 'I am dangerous and living with me could be dangerous.' Thereby confirming for her all the stuff she's been telling her friends he isn't; dark, monosyllabic, mysterious in not a good way.

Having made a series of decisions about which stories are going somewhere and which stories are going nowhere, he has still failed to work out where exactly to go with Anna when she arrives at his door.

He lets her in and takes her into his soothing, blue-lit living room, blue because it satirises boys in blue, one of which he once wanted to be before he decided to go for the bad guys by his rules not theirs, and blue for another reason he tells no one about. She looks around her admiringly, as she tends to do when she comes to his flat; to his astonishment, she thinks he has a 'cultivated sense of décor' and 'a taste for minimalism,' which is mostly because he's never seen the point of acquiring much furniture when there's only him in the flat. But he does like it immaculately clean, after some of the places of his youth; perhaps that cleanliness is another interesting contradiction in her ideas about large, silent men.

Almost immediately after she sits down, his phone sets off its Irish pipes, the music of his childhood, and he makes a regretful face towards her as he picks up the phone, takes it through to the kitchen and presses the record button.

'You have had your warning,' says a half-mechanical, weary sounding voice. It is clearly a recorded message. 'Move at least two hundred miles from this area and stay away for at least a year. If you do not move within a week, or return within the year, we will kill you.'

He goes to Anna. She is sitting on the sofa, thumbing through the latest edition of the paper.

'Anything urgent?' she says.

'No, nothing,' he growls back.

'I love coming here, Ian,' she says, pushing herself back on the sofa. She is the only person in the world, apart from his parents, who calls him 'Ian.' 'So relaxed, so laid back. I'm going to like living with one person rather than three. They're all nice, of course, it's just they're in my face all the time.'

He coughs, and wrenches the words out of him with his own internal forceps.

'It might not be so easy for you to move in, Anna, just at the moment.'

Her eyes search his face. She thought she had understood, but the enigma of him is part of his attraction.

'I thought we'd worked all this out. Are you having second thoughts now?'

He thinks on his feet.

'It's going to take time and organisation, Anna. You getting your stuff here, sorting the place out to take it in. It's time I haven't got at the moment. Work is hectic.'

She plays for time.

'Obviously we need to talk a little more. I'll make some coffee.'

As she makes the coffee, she adjusts the kitchen door so that she can see him. He is sitting forward, his hands on his knees, an oddly outsized ghoulish figure in his blue light. Yes, he is self-contained, but he is sometimes, as now, deeply angry. He contains all emotions, even rage, in his blue place. Something has happened to make him so angry, and that something isn't her. She has seen his eyes on her in the blue light, eyes of desire, intense, needy eyes, but still contained.

He has told her something of his life, ever since appearing in her classroom, her six-year-olds' eyes wide with wonder, as if this figure had walked straight out of one of their giants' stories. The office had, as usual, mistimed matters and sent him to her almost fifteen minutes before the lesson was due to end.

She'd thought he would stand there glowering and frightening them, but within five minutes of coming in, he was talking easily to the kids and they to him; in quarter of an hour, he had formed a team with her. Yes, he was good-looking; yes, he was large and strong, but sinister, threatening, dark-hearted he obviously wasn't.

So what was he doing in his blue room? What kinds of rage did he expect silence and subtle lighting to gobble up? Being Irish in England and English in Ireland? Being big enough to be a suitable target for those wanting to prove their manhood or something? Or was part of it simply being blue, blue as in lonely, blue as in needing someone, blue as a wild animal in a cage condemned to perpetual night?

She sees the envelope on the table with a sheet half sticking out of it. The words 'slit your throat' are clearly visible, and her inhibitions about other people's post

70

immediately disappear. After all, she thinks, she might soon be living here.

By the time she returns to the living room, carrying the coffees and the piece of paper, he knows what has happened.

'Is this why, Ian? You don't want to risk me as well as you?'

'Yes, now you know. Of course it is.'

Forty minutes later, he chills with a beer in his blue light. He has bought a little time. As soon as the threat is neutralised, the move will happen. In the meantime, and this is where they got dangerously close to a row, he must stay where he is. If he is being watched, moving will just shift the problem elsewhere.

It is in such moments, when something good happening is once again taken from his grasp, that he cannot stop his mind returning to where it does not want to go, as if there is some kind of inevitable logic to piling sadness on top of frustration.

The big, yellow, merciless light of a Dublin mortuary, lighting up the tall, slight figure of an eighteen-year-old boy, watching with his guts in his boots as a body slides out of a nearby drawer, the body of the legendary Declan Conroy, Inspector Conroy of Dublin, scourge of all who resort to criminality whatever their politics or affiliations, now pale but for the dried blood stains on his face and neck.

The boy can see his refection in the metal units surrounding him, a gangling, red-eyed, wild-haired mess of a youth.

'I'm sorry, son, and all praise to you for saving your mother from this. Could you please confirm for me that this is your father, Inspector Declan Conroy?'

'Yes, sir,' croaks the boy, while he vows in his heart and stomach never to burn in such a yellow light again.

71

The man's heart tells him he needs to say something.

'You'll hate the world, so you will, Ian. But accidents happen, lad. Brakes will fail.'

'This wasn't an accident, sir. You know that as well as I do.'

The man sighs. But even his best intentions cannot make him disagree. Inspector Conroy has got across some of the biggest bandits in the neighbourhood; giving a terrified local garage owner the choice of tinkling with a few brakes or having his head shot off is not too difficult a choice for him to make.

Even now, in his blue light with his beer to his lips, a few tears can still fill his eyes. Even after his delving and hunting, working with the local paper, into who did the car service, who ordered it, who threatened who, built him a whole folio to hand over to the police, there could still be quiet moments in the blue, with his guts back in his boots, his brain being seared again by the big yellow light.

'You've got him, son. With what you've given us and what we've already got, he'll go down at last. But he's got friends on the inside and out. Your mother will have got a handsome pension. Get her and you out of the country and don't leave tracks...even his bloody writ doesn't run in England.'

So to police school, his determination to do it for Declan outweighing his distaste for all the marching and saluting bullshit, until he remembered that it wasn't marching and saluting which found the man who killed his father, it was journalistic leg work, talking to people who knew people, bugging when he had to, acting the young simpleton when he needed to, those were the weapons which did the job. And so to the press, and hunting villains down, steadily, day by day, bringing them out like vampires into sunlight and watching them frizzle up. And back to chill in the blue, the inner fire eased by a cold sluice of blue and beer.

But, sooner or later, he had to have someone to douse the fire and ultimately put it out, because he knew it would eventually consume him, eat him from the inside out, if he didn't find someone brave enough to take it on. And maybe, just maybe, now he had.

Anna sits thoughtfully in the middle of her afternoon art class, and even though she knew twenty-two six-year-olds will not leave her alone for long to think about anything else but them, she is thinking all the same. She hates being out of her depth, she hates being impotent in something which touches her so closely. Who was hard or foolhardy enough to threaten a six foot five Irish reporter with a gift for investigation and invective? And what possible contribution could a young primary school teacher make to the situation?

It dawns on her that one of the reasons why she is able to think is because of the quietness of the class, the quietness, at the moment, of absorbed children, including, it seems, one or two who generally struggle to become absorbed in anything. Her eyes settle in particular on one of the perpetual physical and chaotic presences, little Josh Briggs; his attention is totally on what he's doing, which is incredibly unusual. He has even gathered to him two of his noisy and distracted friends.

She walks slowly across to him, approaching from behind so as not to interrupt. He has cut out and pasted five letters from the old newspapers available:

KILL U

She cannot stop her noisy intake of breath; he jumps and turns round. He has a leering, unhealthy face for such a young child, and she notices the top of a scar on his back.

'Josh, for heaven's sake! Why have you put that?'

'My dad does this,' he says indignantly, as if asserting an entitlement.

'Josh. How do you know that?'

'He's got a little room next to his office in the garage. Like I get a clout if I go in there. But me and Tommy Banks cut a hole in the floor over it so we could see down. He's going to kill... it says...you can't do anything....'

Josh grins around him, showing once again the lamentable state of his teeth. That and the scar convinces Anna to mention him again to Sheila Dawson, the social worker for his area. But even her concern for him cannot stop a feeling of gratitude and privilege surging through her. She suspects it is nothing like evidence which would stand up in a court of law, even if evidence could be taken from a child testifying against his father. But it is a big, fat pointer, like the ones they used to direct people on the school carnival day.

With the materials put away and the class gone, Anna reaches for her phone. And even as she does, an idea strikes her as if sprung fully formed from the loins of the recent past.

Harry Briggs takes both the paper and the envelope into his inner sanctum, the office at the end of the garage. He has lived with disturbing moments for some time, but this one is the oddest and the most unsettling of them so far.

He makes sure the door is locked and unfolds the sheet on his desk. It is made up of letters cut from newspapers, and it says:

HOW ARE YOU AT ARTWORK, HARRY?

Harry doesn't know what it means, and he doesn't like not knowing. For all the man said about not contacting him directly, this needed something doing about it, and now.

He dials a number which he hasn't been allowed to keep in his contact list, but which he knows well enough.

Fortunately, it is the man himself, rather than one of his inarticulate minions.

'Syerson. Who's this?'

'It's Harry Briggs, Mr. Syerson.'

'Oh, yes? I have said in the past not to phone me directly, Mr. Briggs, haven't I?'

'Yes, I know, sir, but something's come up. Someone seems to know about...about the message I sent.'

'Oh? And how do you know that?'

Harry describes the piece of paper he's received.

'I see,' Syerson says quietly. A very unpanicky man; Harry almost admires him at times.

'And that's not all. I've had a plain clothes cop round here, DS Mansell, he said. Just sniffing about. 'Routine check-up, Harry, just to see everything tickety-boo and above board. Nothing to worry about if you haven't got anything to worry about. Have you got anything to worry about, Harry?' Smarmy get. I'm not sure it's best to go through with it at the moment, Mr. Syerson. Might we let him stew for a bit?'

'Men like Conroy don't stew, Harry. They investigate, they sniff around. Two more weeks and he could be right on your trail, especially after what you've told me. We'll have to act now, as in straight away, as in tonight.'

Jack Pelham stops the recording and looks across at DS Doug Mansell with the air of an uncle greeting a long lost nephew.

'It's clear as a bell, isn't it, Doug. Where did you put the bug?'

'Little shelf next to the phone. You've got to be able to hear it close up. He let me get on checking his paperwork. I told him it would take a while; he was talking to some punter at the time. The next bit is the clincher.'

He re-starts the recording.

'Tonight? I don't know about tonight, Mr. Syerson...'

'Look, Briggs, this was and is a simple enough proposition. Your garage is bust, you want me to bail it out, as you say you support my organisation and will become a full member of it as soon as this is done. You go with a couple of my chaps who know what they're doing, in the small hours of course, so the CCTV can't see damn all. You chuck a tear gas grenade through his window; he's got to come out of the front door, there's no other exit. When he does, you whack his head with the baseball club, and my lead chap will do the knife work. Get out of it, straight back in the van, drive to your garage, change the number plates, burn the club, bury the knife. You don't touch him at any time, not him, not his coat or whatever he's wearing, no prints left anywhere. Even if you don't kill him, you'll frighten the fuck out of him, big as he is. And you'll get him off my bloody back.'

'Can't I leave it to your guys, Mr. Syerson? They're the real professionals here.'

'No, I want you in it, Briggs. If I'm going to bail out your bent garage, you can at least work your passage. I want you and your garage. I can just as easily get my guys to do a job on you, Briggs. Blow you and your fucking garage to kingdom come, you little toerag.'

'Alright, don't get upset, Mr. Syerson. I'm just getting the details clear in my mind.'

'Good. My guys and the van will be with you at three a.m. Just get it done, Briggs.'

With a thumping in his chest which seemed all the noisier for the quietness of the house, Harry Briggs sets out for his garage at 2.30. He backs his car on to the road and then checks his boot to see he has what he needs; he has no intention of leaving any of it visible on the back seat.

He is about to climb back into the driving seat when a slight noise distracts him and he looks up to see a little face at the window. Josh is watching him balefully, even a little suspiciously, it seems, as if Josh had some idea of what his father is about. Harry dismisses the idea as ridiculous – how could he? – and makes himself smile at the boy, even though the chest thumping will not go away.

Josh tries to return the smile, but then he shakes his head sadly, as if asking his dad not to go. A cold fear makes Harry pause at this, but he waves it from him and climbs into his car.

At the garage, the van arrives, with three men in it, though only one, the driver, is visible. Harry takes his balaclava and his baseball club from his boot and climbs into the back of the van, where two men, similarly head-covered and black-clothed, do no more than nod slightly at him.

They park the van behind some trees on a patch of land about half a mile from Conroy's block of flats, and keeping away from the street lights, hurry towards it. The idea is to run there, do the deed and run back, but Harry knows he is overweight and out of condition, and the thumping heart is thumping all the more as soon as he has run a few yards. He remembers his ambitions, so absurd now, that he would one day be a champion boxer; all that gym work and sweat, all those impossible day dreams, all come to nothing, as he stumbles along dressed all in black, the colour of death, on his way to murder a man.

His two companions – the driver has remained in the van – look back with mounting irritation at the slow figure behind them.

'Harry! Shift yourself, for fuck's sake! This has to be quick!'

Harry hears the words half-spat at him and he tries to speed up, but the thumping heart now seems to be converting itself to something much more emphatic, as if it's saying, if you don't take any notice of that, take notice of this. There is suddenly nothing else but an enormous pain, across the chest, the shoulders and the back, and Harry is poleaxed to the ground as if assaulted with his own baseball club. By now the other two are far ahead, and he is spared no more than a glance as they speed on.

In the few minutes left to him, Harry hears a sound of smashing glass, followed by a lot of shouting, much more than could possibly be caused by just two men. The last thing Harry ever sees is a long, sleek police car, parked discreetly down a side street no more than a hundred yards from the block of flats.

Increasingly anxious behind the trees, the van driver leaves after an hour and a half, when none of his companions return. No-one finds Harry until an early morning jogger moves tentatively towards him to establish whether he is drunk or unconscious, and by then it is already much too late.

The dawning light gradually distinguishes details in the living room, catching the upturned newspaper with its banner headline THE GARAGE MAN AND THE NAZI, Exclusive by Ian Conroy. The Syerson/Briggs tale is told in some detail, but with the contribution of little Josh Briggs taken out. It has been easy enough to single out Conroy's former article on Briggs as his motivation, with the supporting evidence of the bugged conversation. The part played by Josh's teacher is also missing, with her approval.

In the main bedroom, the subdued blue meets the dawn silver to pick out two naked human bodies like ethereal avatars, beautiful in their sleep, the man's long, defined back next to the woman's embryonic shape, curves and undulations to the man's angles and edges. Love-making has fed and given way to rest, for the time being at least, though soon they will both wake and then, oblivious to the panoramic skyline of the city which makes the window a spectacular background, they will make love again, to greet a day which both of them have as leisure time.

However, the leisure time will include transferring Anna's belongings from her shared house to her new home. The replaced and reinforced front window has been accompanied by several other security measures, paid for by Conroy's employers at the urging of editor Jack, who can be as assertive towards his paper's tycoon lordship owner as he is with the paper's employees.

'Sooner or later, Tom, one of the national dailies will make him an offer he can't refuse. In the meantime, he's my main man and I intend to treat him like it. He does the business, and if he's out there getting shot at, he has to have some ammunition in his own locker. He's a weird bugger in some ways; he lights his place in blue like some kind of Scandinavian knocking shop, and he speaks about one sentence an hour, but he's the real deal, and that's all I'm bothered about.'

Conroy wakes and watches her as she breathes easily and stretches an arm towards him. He closes his eyes, and at last, there are no more bright yellow lights.

WHITE LIES AND CARNIVALS

I am in my Uncle Peter's study, dark wood and plain blue carpet, and Aunt Mary is in the garden below. I can see her moving between her greenhouse and her plant beds. The shape of her is so familiar to me that I can almost interpret her mood at a glance. At the moment, she moves as if moving is an effort in itself; she is sixty-eight years old, so perhaps it is, but there is a fragility now, a vulnerability, inevitable when someone loses their lifelong spouse.

She married Uncle Peter when she was twenty years old, and they were already making plans for a golden wedding anniversary when Uncle Peter, heading back six weeks ago from one of the literary festivals he so liked, had a heart attack at the wheel of his car and was dead not long after he'd swerved down a bank at the side of the road.

My name is Marcus Welby; my surname is the maiden name of the lady pottering around below. She is my father's elder sister. He is generally devoted to her, but I discovered in adulthood that he worries about her 'naivete, Marcus, is the only word for it, quite honestly. Mary is generous to a fault, friendly and outgoing, but she is not difficult to get round and people can do it too easily. I know, I've done it, God forgive me, and I was only a thoughtless whelp at the time; what a more artful deceiver might achieve has always worried me.'

I came into this confidence after I had effectively become 'the family lawyer.' Ever since qualifying, after interminable years of articled training, exams and tea-boying in chambers, the confidences thrust upon me have become a niggling irritant, not least because of a widespread assumption that every lawyer is an expert in every kind of law, which few are.

However, in this case, my probate speciality has finally caught me out. Even though he was seventy years old, Uncle Peter hadn't made a will, and Aunt Mary wouldn't have been the one to insist that he did. In such circumstances, the spouse inherits, but what she will inherit is another matter; a fortune or a mountain of debt? My father considers Peter's failure to make a will typical of the man; he describes Peter to me, inelegantly, as 'not of this world. I'm not sure which world he is of, but it isn't this bloody one.'

Uncle Peter was a lecturer by profession, a man steeped in highbrow literature. My father, as even he would admit, is not. It is my aunt's supposed naivete and my uncle's apparent unworldliness which has landed me in this uncomfortable position. This room has always been forbidden ground. Peter could even get tetchy with Mary if she ventured into this place; for nephews, it was strictly forbidden. I feel like a sinner invading the temple.

But, being an obedient son and a helpful nephew, even as forty looms ever closer, I allowed my mother to inveigle me into 'sorting out Peter's affairs, please, darling,' sitting on stools on either side of the island in the kitchen where all serious family matters are thrashed out.

'Have we asked Aunt Mary?' I offer tentatively, writhing like a fish on the end of Mother's line. Two audible tuts. Two are bad news; three are crisis point.

'Of course we've asked Mary, Marcus. For heaven's sake. Did you honestly think you could just go there and examine Peter's study without asking Mary? Obliging she may be, but not that obliging. She knows next to nothing about what's in that study, and as she says herself, she probably wouldn't understand it anyway. As far as your

81

father and I can make out, Peter retained total control of all their finances, and you know well enough what your father thinks of Peter's grasp of worldly affairs. If they are deep in debt or have made disastrous investments, we can't just leave Mary to it, Marcus. And in this matter, my dear boy, you are the only one of us who really knows what he's talking about.'

Perhaps the sheer gratification of hearing that smothered my further protests. One of my current briefs was a case of a multi-millionaire who had also died intestate, with at least five different parties fighting over the spoils, including the couple I represent. It promises to be of Dickensian proportions in terms of time and complexity, and here I am distracted from one labyrinth to another, right on my doorstep. However, as my father was all too prone to observe, when I returned home limping from rugby, or having broken up with a girlfriend, or having drunk too much the night before etc. etc., 'into each life a little rain must fall, old lad.' It's no wonder I have acquired the ability to curse silently.

As I am doing while sifting through Uncle Peter's keys and fearing, even then, his magisterial self suddenly materialising beside me. Not that he was an angry man; somewhat to the contrary, in fact. His studied calm was legendary and perhaps the real irritant for my father. Aunt Mary was headmistress of an infant school for many years; her skills with her children, which, a long time ago, included me, were a pleasure to experience then and watch later. When she was reading a story, the only audible noise would be her mellifluent voice, including every accent and emphasis the story needed.

Every year, the school would have a Carnival – yes, with a capital C – with stalls, games, pastimes, exhibits of work, a thorough snapshot of the work and fun the school enjoyed. Uncle Peter always took the day off from his more elevated university to help out, and, whatever my father says, help out in very practical ways, ferrying furniture and materials about and helping set up tents and stalls etc.

Those Carnivals, with their feasts of fun, laughter and colour, remain set like gems in the canvas of my childhood, and I went on helping out with them even after leaving the school, until adolescence led me into naughtier but no less entertaining pursuits. And here I am being churlish about helping out my poor aunt. Perhaps I deserve a smack; perhaps, sometimes, I did then, but it wouldn't have come from Aunt Mary. 'No child goes to school to be assaulted, Marcus,' she once said to me. I reflected on that when my father made his comment; perhaps naivete, if that's what it is, has its virtues.

Forty minutes after beginning my inspection, I am heartened and encouraged. Uncle Peter had generous sums in various accounts and investments, and certainly enough to keep Aunt Mary in comfort for the rest of her life, which will hopefully be some years yet. I can see her working intently now on a bed of flowers which looks colourful and flourishing, capable of consoling her simply by being there. She is absorbed, her hands moving expertly and her eyes taking in every detail. A sudden intense gratitude sweeps through me, not too frequent an experience in my line of work. I will soon be able to put her mind at rest, at least on the material issues.

I am starting to lock everything again when something jumps out at me, so obviously that it cannot be ignored. My business inevitably makes me aware of furniture structures, and I have seen this model of bureau before. It contains a 'secret' compartment and I knew the sequence of presses and pushes which would open it.

Cursing inwardly again, I am seriously tempted to leave it unopened. Let sleeping dogs lie, another favourite of my father's. But it could be something which negates or compromises everything else, and neglect in this kind of case, especially one so close to home, has a habit of striking back.

Sure enough, a recess is revealed, and it is full almost to the brim with papers and some photographs. What is perhaps worse, most of the papers look personal rather than official. I pick up one in my uncle's recognisable handwriting, and it takes only three words to disconcert me. 'My darling Luke,' the letter begins.

My delving entirely absorbs my attention for the next hour. The photos include one of two young men, no more than nineteen or twenty, in skimpy swimming trunks, and several other scantily-clad beach or rural shots. The letters, conveniently kept in chronological order, speak frankly about the sexual nature of the relationship. My discomfort grows, not because of homophobia, but because my presence in this study has now moved beyond investigative to invasive, as it tells me things I don't need to know.

And yet, my lawyer self says I probably do need to know, in the interests of my aunt. She does not seem to be mentioned much in the letters at all, and certainly there are no cheap or disparaging remarks. Peter says at one point that 'Mary finds any kind of sexual activity distasteful; it makes demands on her she is unable to meet.' All the same, I cannot think Mary knew about this, and even if the deception is well-motivated, the scale of it is disturbing and quite breath-taking.

There are pictures of Peter and Luke with literary figures, both writers and poets, some of whom even my less literary self can recognise; there are literary festival programmes with either my uncle or his friend Luke

Glaister making contributions to the line-up. I remember asking Aunt Mary once why she didn't go with her husband to more of these occasions.

'I would be a bit out of my depth, dear,' she said, followed by that slightly naughty, conspiratorial smile she had, which will be one of my abiding memories of her.

'That's the official line, anyway, Marcus. To be honest, dear, I do get ' – her voice faded to a whisper – 'just a teeny bit bored.'

The autumn dusk is beginning to set in; Aunt Mary has moved into the greenhouse. The noises emerging from it are disjointed, as if she is trying to keep herself occupied while mulling everything over. I realise I have now been in this study for nearly two hours. I know I will be staying for dinner; we both knew this was bound to take a while, and my wife and family are not expecting me home until later. Aunt Mary will soon be starting to put the meal together, and I would normally relish the prospect of it; she uses fresh ingredients from the garden and she is a very good cook. However, this might be the one which could stick in my throat a little.

It suddenly dawns on me that I knew Luke Glaister. The tall man with blondish hair and piercingly alive light blue eyes, who had a slight stoop and was always introduced as an 'old family friend and boyhood chum.' Mary's own comment about him comes back to me; 'oh, yes, he and Luke go way, way back; schooldays, university, now both lecturers. Mutually supportive, and a good thing for Peter. Friendships which stand the test of time are always valuable; I have one or two myself.'

Which led me into another series of wild conjectures. The familial ground is moving beneath my feet. How staid and set the young always think their elders to be, while a whole panoply of adult life carries on behind the pedestrian façade.

Aunt Mary moves out of the greenhouse carrying a couple of bags to take to the kitchen. As she passes below the window, I see her face look upwards, and the anxiety there is plain to see. I move over and open the window.

'Won't be long now, Aunt Mary,' I say, wondering at the bland assertion my voice can manage. 'Nothing very problematic, but lots of red tape, as there always is.'

The way her face breaks into relief makes me both grateful and self-critical; in the circumstances, it's been a long time not to give her any information.

And the very moment I close the window and turn to look down to one of the pictures of Peter and Luke gazing at the camera, a memory comes back to me very powerfully of a seemingly inconsequential incident which had lasting meaning in my life.

It was my last holiday with my parents, to a resort we often went to in Devon, not far from where Peter and Mary lived. They had joined us for the day. I was standing right on the shore, balanced on one hip, like boys do; I was sixteen coming on to seventeen. The trunks I had on were probably even skimpier than the ones worn by Peter and Luke when they were not much more than boys. Because they'd been a gift, I felt obliged to wear them, but whoever had given me them hadn't accounted fully for my rapid growth and to me, a rather retiring youth in such matters, they verged on the indecent.

Entranced by the sky, the air and the spectacular blue of the sea, I stood there for several minutes, I suppose. When I turned, I saw Uncle Peter and his friend Mr. Glaister gazing towards me like they gazed into the camera for the picture in the study. Peter wore the benevolent smile he always wore in my direction – he was never anything but kind, even indulgent, towards me – but there was something else about it, especially when accompanied by Mr. Glaister, something assessing, perhaps even admiring, in a way which wasn't entirely avuncular. It flustered me, and just as my eyes turned from him, I saw there were a group of girls, probably none of them older than fifteen, whose eyes were also on me, and there was nothing ambiguous in those looks at all.

Now embarrassed to the core, I plunged off into the water for a ten-minute swim, stoically ignoring its temperature, then I ran back to my parents and a covering towel. But the point had been made in my mind; I was clearly no longer a child, and some people might actually now find me physically attractive. The fact that they might include my uncle and his friend was largely thrust away by the girls, and only now re-emerges, as I find myself in both my uncle's study and life more than I really want to be.

I put everything gathered out of this secret compartment into my bag; the other stuff can wait. Aunt Mary will not be surprised that a second visit will be necessary. The chances of her finding this material are very slim indeed, but I intend to make them non-existent, for the moment at least.

As I'm collecting the last papers, I notice the most recent date, and a letter looking much more official than most of them. It was also dated some years after the last written letter, from Peter to Luke. It was a classic lawyer kind of letter, saying what it needed to say at unnecessary length, but it managed to answer my nagging curiosity about why Peter, oddly, had his letters both from and to Luke.

Luke Glaister, it seemed, had died alone only three weeks before Peter's heart attack. Their correspondence had dried up nearly ten years earlier. Luke had lost the sister he lived with after her long term illness. Luke had asked, or begged almost, for Peter to leave his wife and come to him. Peter said no. While the coroner's verdict on Luke was accidental death, an autumnal swimming incident, suspicions remained that it had effectively been suicide. Only the lawyer's final paragraph allowed any emotion to creep in.

'Mr. Glaister made clear to me when, rather unexpectedly, he decided to make a full and final Will two years ago, that all his correspondence with you should be returned to you personally; he wanted nothing about his relationship with you to finish up 'in the public domain,' as he called it, or to be made available to people with 'bad motive.' He is also returning to you the St. Christopher which you gave him when he was 25 to keep him safe. As he does not feel able to say so directly to you, he has asked me to tell you, in so many words, that he loves you and always has done.'

By the end of the letter, I can hardly see it for embarrassing moisture. Sooner or later, I suppose, the St. Christopher will be found amongst Peter's belongings, and a question mark will hang over that; however he was at the age of twenty five, Peter wasn't a religious man in his later years. My experience has led me to being involved in various acrimonious and damaging family disputes, and I can only guess at what effect this might have on my aunt if she should ever know.

I try to make myself ready to go down and dine with Aunt Mary, and I will do my best to enjoy the superb meal she will put before me. Truth and justice are the business of lawyers, but they both share one ubiquitous characteristic; they amount only to whatever each person or individual defines them to be. My uncle lived a lie, thoroughly and no doubt at times very painfully. At least some notions of truth would call it a white lie, and at least some notions of justice would call it as fair to all concerned as anything could be in such a situation, which isn't very much.

My memories will stay with the Carnivals, when life was simple and fun, and my uncle and aunt did their best to keep it that way for all of us.

THE LADY AT THE STATION

Trains through Brent Stanwick Station are frequent; trains that stop are not. They are twice a day, and one is due in half an hour. More or less. Strict punctuality is not the network's prime characteristic.

Nothing to be done, then, except languish about enjoying the country air. That's pretty much why I come to Brent Stanwick occasionally. I'm not complaining; I chose the Smoke when the opportunity arose, rather than stay with regional papers. I like the buzz of London, and seeing my name on something I've written, not so rare now.

Brent Stanwick. is a model village, a Miss Marple thing, with a church, a pub, a shop and not much else. It's also the home of my Aunt Alice, my father's elder sister, for whom I have a real soft spot. She is a gentler character than either of my parents, though she hasn't, of course, had the dubious pleasure of bringing me up.

Me being Edward Stilgow, Ed, reporter tasked with digging up secrets and nosing out stories, a profession which suits my restless, nosey and sometimes aggressive nature. 'It's like having a permanently sore tooth,' was how my one of my exes summed it up.

Whatever. Hacks don't need to be nice guys. But sometimes I escape to Brent Stanwick, to eat cake and sip tea with Aunt Alice and spend a peaceful noiseless night, not something London's good at. Brent Stanwick is only about thirty-five minutes by train from London. All of us need our Brent Stanwicks.

I'm also enjoying the station on my own, or rather, I thought it was, until I sense, somewhere near my nosey hack nose, a lady sitting on a bench about fifty yards away on my right. Nice coat, unhatted, fiftyish, once pretty, maybe not that long ago. I smile, I nod, the day wears on.

However, an odd phenomenon now becomes obvious enough to be undeniable. The woman is staring at me.

Now, no false modesty here; I am twenty five, a regular gym goer, as good-looking as I'll ever be. But walking sex magnet? Home counties hunk? Moi? So attractive that a mature lady can do nothing but stare in wonder?

I don't think so, and a few seconds later, all becomes a little less mysterious. We have another male personage in our midst, and it's him she's staring at, though why she would stare at him is as mysterious as why she would stare at me. He looks much like me; same sort of build, similar height, but perhaps with a year or two added on. But neither the lady nor I have any meaning in his life, apparently. He is clicking away on his phone; the lady and I might just as well be lamp posts as far as he's concerned.

This is the Brent Stanwick equivalent of the rush hour. I sneak a glance back towards herself, and now she really is staring at me. And suddenly, she speaks.

'You haven't heard, have you?' Clipped and sharp, rather teacherish.

This kind of statement is usually bad news, but the sort you need to know when standing on train platforms. She points wordlessly at the arrivals board, which has a tiny 'cancelled' sign, eventually visible from about six inches away. And yes, it is referring to my train.

I let loose an uninhibited expletive before remembering that uninhibited expletives should not be uttered near middle-aged ladies. I glance at her intending to apologise, but she just says 'my sentiments precisely. Some nonsense about maintenance work on the line. It's always something or other, isn't it?'

91

Now I have a problem – the next train is five hours away, and I have an appointment with an editor in just over two hours, and he's the kind of guy you don't want to be too late for if you're intending to stay in his employ.

However, there doesn't seem much to be done about it but phone him and tell him the bad news, after which I will reconcile myself to yet more tea and cake with Aunt Alice, not exactly a fate worse than death, but then the lady's tone changes suddenly. It is tense, urgent, almost pleading.

'Don't go, please. For a few minutes at least. Sit here for a minute, please.'

Two pleases will do, I think, especially with a sudden five-hour gap to fill. I sit on the bench. At close quarters, she seems quite formidable, the kind of teacher you'd think twice about flicking pellets at, in case she comes back and shoves them straight up your nose.

'That man standing there is looking to kill me. As long as you're around, he probably won't. He's a professional; he doesn't like witnesses.'

During the course of this astonishing speech, I become conscious of two facts. One, the bench is wetter than it seemed, and cold streams of moisture are making their way across my trousered bottom just as cold fears sneak over my heart. Secondly, I can already, as a journalist, identify crucial words, and the one in her sentence is 'probably.'

'Who is he?' I hear my little voice say, like a bleat in the mist.

'Oh.' Gesture of impatience. 'He's an agent.'

'What – a bookie? A theatrical?'

A quick, daggerish look, as if I'm heading for the naughty step.

'He's a double agent, posing as one of ours.'

I swallow a sudden urge to run, fast and far. She is either insane or something quite heavy is going down here. Either way is far outside my comfort zone.

She looks me up and down, seemingly noticing me properly for the first time.

'What do you do?' she says.

'I'm a journalist.'

'Oh, God.'

'No, Ed. Ed Stilgow. How do you do?'

She ignores my hand.

'Nothing I tell you can be splashed all over any newspaper.'

'O.K., if you say so. Just as long as we don't both finish up splashed all over this bench.'

She looks towards our friend at the end of the platform to our left, blocking us from the car park. He remains absorbed in his phone; he looks like he's playing online dominoes or something. Perhaps he hasn't heard about the cancelled train, but I'm not in the running to inform him just at the moment.

She motions me to move closer, as if commanding me to come to her desk.

'I can't say more at the moment, other than I have been investigating him for some time and he knows I have blown his cover.'

'I can see how he might have a grudge.'

Her voice rose.

'He has been playing a dangerous game, trying to play both sides at once, but I know well enough what he's up to.'

I glance at our friend again. Not a flicker. Still absorbed in clicking away.

'He tailed me in his car. I thought I'd shake him off and take the train, rather than have him tailing me all the way to London.'

'Why don't you phone someone for help?'

A kind of exasperated dagger look this time.

'Because, by the time they came to my aid, he would probably have killed me. He is a very good shot.'

I looked to my left again. Just a glance, now returned, but then again, why wouldn't it be, when the only two people anywhere near him keep looking at him?

I sigh. Brent Stanwick was never this. Brent Stanwick is tea, cake and Aunt Alice. And Miss Marple. Whodunits were a passion of mine. I aimed to be either a detective or a journalist; some people would say that there's not a lot to choose between them.

'How on earth did you both fetch up in Nether Stanton?'

'He followed me on the motorway. His persistence has persuaded me that he knows, somehow, what I've got on him. I came off at the most obscure junction I knew; I thought I was far enough in front for him not to see. Then I realised what a fool I'd been; he had a tracker on my car. He's like that. I told you, he's a professional. He suddenly appeared on the platform just two minutes before you did. If you hadn't appeared, he might already have started shooting.'

I try to think of something; I'm a hack, aren't I, endlessly resourceful?

'I've got a phone in my pocket. I'll try to get help.'

'No!' she says, too loudly. Then her voice falls.

'Don't make a movement into your pocket, please.'

'Oh, to hell –' I start to say, thinking either the police or men in white coats would do, what should I care, then there's a loud click on concrete and as I turn to my left, his eyes are full on and they are disturbing eyes, intense, dark brown eyes, and his hand is in his coat pocket.

Journalists always talk about stories. Sometimes they confuse stories with real life. This is the moment of changeover for me. I'd seen the guy full in the eyes.

And suddenly, believe it or not, I get a jolt of real life courage, like a bravery jab.

'What's your name?' I whisper to her.

'Phyllis. Phyllis will do.'

'What's his?'

'Whatever he's currently using, which could be anything, though I know him as Karl.'

'Well, Phyllis, we're going to walk slowly off this platform, with my arm round you so he can't separate his target. If his hand takes something out of his pocket, we will both make a hell of a noise and run for it. If he doesn't, we'll make our way back to your car, and I'll call for help as you drive away. O.K.?'

'Yes. And thank you.'

And, at this point, further inspiration strikes; I turn on my body camera, a useful little journalistic piece of kit hidden strategically in my coat. Then I throw my arm around Phyllis and smile at the guy; he daggers me again. I smile back, partly because I now have him on film, should he decide to loose off at us. I nod down at the camera to make him aware of this. I might be dead, but he'll be doing life. Somehow, it only goes so far as a consolation.

We inch our way along the platform and he edges his way behind us, but at least he is behind us. A few feet at a time, gently as you like, never fully turning our backs.

'Talk to me,' I say, or rather whisper. 'He needs to believe this is natural.'

Both my hands and my back are sweating, my hands because of fear, my back because of the expectation of a heavy slug landing in it. We continue edging slowly forward, until an unfamiliar voice sounds in the near-silence; the voice of the man watching us, and rather than a sinister foreign accent with East European undertones, he sounds solid Smoke.

'I am a plain-clothes policeman. This woman has escaped from a mental institution some miles from here. If you carry on, you will be guilty of obstructing the police in the execution of their duty. Please move away from the woman.'

And I see, out of the corner of my eye, that he really does have a gun pointing in our direction; it's mostly concealed by his hand, but it's there alright.

'He will say or do anything now to convince you,' the woman says, and the tone of her voice speaks of fear clearly enough.

I disentangle my tongue from the back of my mouth; my throat is parched.

'This institution you speak of,' I manage to say. 'It usually rounds up stray patients at gunpoint, does it?'

'It is if they are known to be dangerous,' he says. As answers go, this is probably up there with all good conversation stoppers. I cannot help but look down at the lady's face, close to mine. I'm trying to deduce what character is lurking behind this convincing pale, vulnerable face, that nevertheless has a steel in the eyes which she cannot easily hide, whatever the rest of her expression is doing.

We continue to edge along the platform, the lady and I. My reserves of courage have not yet exhausted themselves, but there's undoubtedly quite a serious leakage going on. I think a little old-fashioned sarcasm might help me along.

'I'll be careful,' I say, 'in case she gets me with her handbag.'

He's not amused.

'That woman,' he says evenly, 'could kill you with a single blow. I'm not carrying this gun just for the hell of it.'

Herself seems to remain indifferent; she just keeps shuffling along. I try to keep enough presence of mind to think through my options, but I'm only too well aware that, if I did choose to believe him and break away from the woman, only to see her shot down in cold blood, I'd never be able to live with myself. All the stuff in my twenty-five-year-old mind, the supposed worldliness, the glib cynicism about pretences to sincerity, was, I could see, only skin deep.

Slowly, slowly, we shuffle along, with the guy beginning to look gratifyingly bemused himself and suddenly, glory be, there's someone checking the parking tickets in the station car park, which happens in Brent Stanwick about once every five years, so maybe the dice are rolling for us. Now he will have to kill three of us to make sure there are no witnesses, and he doesn't look so sure of himself. His hand, hovering over his pocket, even seems to be shaking a little.

The church, right next to the car park, is in sight now. An elderly couple I vaguely recognise are visiting a grave, and I whisper a silent prayer, which I rarely do – no, I never do – that I will next be in that church yard as a visitor, not an inmate.

She directs me by touch, and goodness knows what we must look like, but she's thinking herself into her part; she's even assumed a slight limp which wasn't there before.

'You are helping your dear old mum to the car, boy, and it had better be convincing,' she mutters at me, and once again, this is the kind of utterance that doesn't sound too little old lady to me.

She mutters a description of her car to me, and suddenly, we are only ten yards from it in a lane next to the church, and it is a more isolated and camouflaged spot as the lane disappears down the side of the graveyard. Phyllis makes a quick lunge for the door, and in a matter of five seconds, I am on my own on the other side of the car.

'Now there will be one warning shot, and then you will both stand beside the car with your hands up,' he says, and there is a click which is unmistakably him clicking off the safety catch on his gun.

In the next second, the passenger door beside me is flung open.

'Get in,' she shouts, 'get in now!'

I get, or rather jump, in, and in another second, his gun lets out a dull thud and a bullet skims the roof of the car. I let out an involuntary shout; Phyllis says nothing. But by the time he's levelling his gun up to have another go, he has to make a rapid dive to his right to stop himself being run over, and within a few more seconds, we are screeching out of Nether Stanton in a display of stunt driving which I doubt whether the place has ever seen before or will ever see again. Nevertheless, within a few miles, as we reach the motorway heading north, there the guy is again, just a few cars behind and making his way carefully up to us.

'Tell me more about yourself,' she says suddenly.

'Ed. Ed Lithgow. Favourite colour green, Capricorn. For God's sake. What does it matter?'

'It keeps us talking. It's important.'

So here I am, in a car with a woman who could, reputedly, kill me with a single blow, having just been shot at by a guy who says the woman is a dangerous lunatic. I suppose I should be saying grateful thanks to whatever patron saint of hacks digs up the stories, but somehow, when you're actually in the story, it isn't so storyish any more. Once again, some voice is asking me to decide who I believe. For the moment, I choose to believe the woman, mainly because she's driving the car. And driving it quite restrainedly, none of your big car chase jobs here.

'Aren't you going to try and get away from him?' I ask.

'Not a lot of point if he's got a tracker on the car, is there? In any case, I'm heading for a road I've used before, when I think I'll have a good chance of shaking him off.'

'O.K.,' I say. 'Let's keep talking then. How do you know he's a double agent?'

'Being an agent is a desperately stressful business,' she says, her eyes still resolutely on the road. 'The wonder of it is that more of them don't go rogue. We thought he was reliable; he'd been on our books for years. When I found out he was betraying us and working for the opposition, I got as much evidence together as I could and eventually I managed to get him out of the Service, while in the teeth of some determined opposition from people, some of them in very high places, who apparently thought that I was the opposition agent, or at least claimed they did.'

'It sounds like some kind of crazy espionage merry-go-round.'

'Yes, that's probably a fair description. Eventually, I was forced into early retirement. I knew then that he, or one of his associates, would come for me, because as long as I'm alive, I have the information to discredit him and his organisation, and he doesn't want to take the risk of my ex-employers having a change of heart.'

'So why didn't he just shoot you when he had the chance?'

'Well, he's a professional. In an isolated spot like Brent Stanwick, where nothing happens from one century to the next, there would be such a commotion and such widespread publicity that he would feel his anonymity threatened. He's more a back alley, lurking in the shadows kind of guy.'

Throughout this time, she is driving quite normally; there's no undue turn of speed, no attempt to shake the guy off. She can see him quite clearly in her rear view mirror, and I can see him in the wing mirror.

'Meaning he won't try on the motorway, presumably?'

'Oh, God, no. Good agents only deal in certainties, or as near certainties as they can get, and they don't invite attention from any of the local law enforcement agencies, even the motorway police.'

'Is he a good agent?'

'Well, he has been, but he started getting a little careless with details, which put me on to him as a double agent, things he wouldn't have done a few years ago. Generally speaking, he thinks on his feet; look at how rapidly he concocted a story about me having escaped from a mental institution. You're still not too sure about that, are you?'

'You're much more convincing as a retired agent than you are as an escaped lunatic. Either way up, it's a hell of a story.'

'Story?' She sounds incredulous; maybe she's forgotten I'm a journalist.

'Yes, story. I write for a paper, remember?'

'You'll never be able to print this, Ed. I'm sorry.'

'Why?'

'Because everyone will deny it. How do you think a secret service stays secret? In any case, you don't even know any names.'

'I know you're Phyllis. Although, there again, you're not, are you?'

'I am today; I'll be someone else tomorrow. Likewise our friend back there.'

I realise how young and naïve I still am. I frown at the wing mirror, and the man with the gun smiles wickedly at me; perhaps he's looking forward to putting a bullet in me, as some kind of revenge upon a simpleton for being a simpleton.

Another thought, obvious as it probably is, just occurs to me.

'Are you aiming to kill that guy?'

'Not unless I have to in self-defence. He's more use to us alive than dead. He's probably carrying some crucial evidence with him in that car; he's not the type to trust to lockers or other supposedly secret hiding places; he likes to have stuff with him. If he's caught in that car, he will try to torch it before anyone can search it. There could well be enough to get him banged up for life as a traitor, though knowing the present hierarchy as I do, they would be more likely to try and turn him again, even though we all know he cannot be trusted further than I can throw him.'

I sit there, sulking, I suppose I have to say, yet I know well enough that this is how most people experience life; if strange things happen around them, whether they have any chance of finding out what's going on is highly unlikely. Being a hack makes you think you're a cut above, you know what's going on, you have the bloodhound equipment to sniff out the realities and distinguish between what people want you to think is happening and what actually is happening. Maybe, if this 'story' had happened later in my career, I would have had better answers, but then, I just had to live with the fact that I was another ordinary Joe, going to see his old aunt for tea and cake, when all this lot came along. Maybe the biggest story I've ever likely to find myself caught up in, and I can't print a word about it.

My glum mood seems to have communicated itself, because when she spoke again, it is as if she was trying to cheer up her favourite nephew.

'Never mind, Ed. Things are going to get more lively very soon.'

My first reaction to this remark is incredulity, bearing in mind that my day had already included a stranger pulling a gun on me in a quiet rural station, and only just getting away from him before he put a bullet in me. Things have already been every bit as lively as I cared for, so I can only speculate, with understandable apprehension, about just what extra liveliness this lady has in mind.

I don't have to wait long. Five minutes after her last remark, she leaves the motorway, and I could see we were now heading for the coast. She makes no attempt to conceal what she's doing or increase her speed; she signals perfectly correctly, and it's almost as if she's inviting our friend to follow her, which, of course, he does.

Three minutes after we hit the coast road – exactly three, because I am looking at my watch, maybe out of a morbid curiosity with the minute when I will finally come to whatever sticky end has been threatening all day – she suddenly bangs her foot down on the accelerator and we're off on what I can only describe as a frantic screech of a drive.

Although, to be strictly accurate, it is me and the car who are doing the screeching; Phyllis, or whatever her name is, remains entirely calm and unruffled, as if she's just taking the motor for a spin. Even when we zoom along a road close to banks leading down into the sea, she remains coolly in control. Bollards, fencing, white lines, cats' eyes, flash by in seconds, sometimes no more than inches away from the edge of the car.

I sit with my pale knuckles clutching on to my seat belt for dear life. I promise whoever that I will for ever after believe in God, that I will even go to church with my aunt and sing along while I share her hymn book, that all the glib, atheistic gibes I've ever come out with were just a boy being a boy, if only divine providence will let me continue my still short life when I'm finally released from this car.

But even in my state of high alarm, I am observant enough to see that, while Phyllis seems to know this road and is anticipating everything coming her way, the guy behind us pretty obviously doesn't. On several occasions, he almost comes to grief, and it is some kind of comfort to know that Phyllis is playing on her home turf here.

We arrive, or more accurately scream over, the top of a hill, and the other side takes the road down past a grassy, rocky promontory about a hundred yards from the water.

'Right!' says Phyllis, and all her previous excesses of speed are as nothing compared to the rate she gets to belting down this long gradual hill. Almost at the bottom, a ridiculously sharp bend suddenly comes into focus; Phyllis knows it's there, and leaves herself just enough time to get round it, even though her tyres are screeching blue murder. The man following obviously doesn't know it's there, and before he can adjust enough, his car is bumping down over the scattered rocks and grassy bits towards the coast, and what that must be doing to his car doesn't take too much of an imagination to work out, let alone how he's being jolted around. Not more than five yards from the water, his car, or what's left of it, slowly grinds to a halt.

103

Phyllis has slowed her car down and she pulls in to a layby at the top of the hill on the other side, where we both get out of the car to see her pursuer with waves lapping at his tyres. I am about to protest that someone needs to go and see how the guy is, or do something, when I hear her on the phone in her car.

I watch with mounting amazement, and I realise my hands are still shaking. After a few minutes, she emerges from the car. I am staring down onto the beach, wondering if the guy down there will ever move again. She joins me, and we stand there like a couple of gawking rubberneckers watching a hanging or something.

'Look,' I say, 'that guy could be seriously hurt. He could be dead. Shouldn't we do something? I know he's Bob the Bandit and all that, but he's still a human being. Or was.'

'I just did do something, Ed. But bear in mind that man is armed and is almost certainly carrying incriminating information in that car. He always has over-estimated his ability to cover his tracks. I don't want anyone removing your body from the beach, or for that matter, mine.'

'But, come on, Phyllis –'

'Just be a little patient, Ed. Ten minutes, I'd guess.'

It shows how much the woman has mesmerised me by this stage that I do as I'm told and shut up. And sure enough, in just under ten minutes, we can see an ambulance moving down the hill, much more carefully than our recent descent. It finds a piece of flat ground to allow it to pull off the road.

And then they just sit and wait. Now we can see a dazed figure, edging painfully out of the crashed car. For a few minutes, the ambulance guys just watch what's happening. Then a tiny black object in the sky gets rapidly closer and reveals itself as a police helicopter.

'The police will tell the ambulance when they think it's safe for them to go to him. For us, Ed, it's time to go.'

'Go?' I say. 'This is getting to the interesting bit.'

She manages a quick flash of a smile.

'They will want me to be a witness, and I haven't got the card with me which would exempt me. The department will have to decide whether or not I can testify. As it is, we need to be out of here before the question arises. Sorry, Ed.'

She drops me at the nearest town with a station and a connection to London. So I manage to make it home without having to explain the events of my day to Aunt Alice; just as well, because I wouldn't know where to start.

All this was in my cub reporter days, nearly twenty five years ago now. As the lady said, I couldn't use the story because I had no proof of it, and no-one involved would talk to me. But it was more than once in the back of my mind that maybe, just maybe, that guy had been right, and Phyllis was actually a lady who had become deranged somehow and had escaped from whoever was looking after her.

Then, a couple of years ago, I saw a picture in a paper. The face was older and greyer; the sharp, dark eyes were mistier and the hair more carefully styled, but it was her alright; it's not a face I can ever forget. I'm not going to say her name, because if I do, I'll have a million spooks all over me denying that she was involved in anything like the events described. But she was a Dame, given an honour 'for services to her country' and one sentence summed up her 'remarkable and tenacious ability to apprehend and neutralise enemy agents.'

I know well enough now the difference between the stories we can tell and the stories we can't, and I've come to regard Phyllis – I'll always think of her as Phyllis – as one of my most valuable instructors, who I happened upon at a quiet rural station just after tea and cakes with Aunt Alice.

A FULL MOON OVER SADIE DEMPSTER'S...

Alan felt ambivalent about returning to live so close to where he was born, the village being clearly visible from his apartment. He suspected it might be a misguided attempt to reconnect a life circle. His wife Anne had died over five years ago, and more or less cut him loose; he'd always talked of 'we,' like royalty.With only one child, a son, now grown up with his own family, he and Anne moved ever closer together, retrieving for themselves a joint identity not defined by roles – journalists, parents, aunts, uncles, grandparents. Alan Nicholson, Anne Nicholson nee Armitage; spending almost all of the time with just the two of them, their understanding of each other prospered. Solitude had already become too devastating a novelty for Alan; he needed to re-root myself somewhere, and he felt there was nowhere else to go but his time before Anne.

The physical realities were disappointing. The stretch of river central to his boyhood, remembered as a spreading rural panorama, now seemed just an untidy, partly overgrown broad bend in a stream. The house behind it, which once towered over it like a gothic castle, was a bed and breakfast establishment, its two large front rooms enhanced, or perhaps defaced, by bolted on metal balconies. It was still, essentially, a mundane Victorian brick construction, with the battlement-like structures on the roof more fussy than mysteriously medieval.

Even so, he felt that the mythology survived the modern realities. The woman who was living in that house in 1944 became a local mythology in herself. Six years before, she had arrived in the community as the wife of Charles Dempster, the second son of Sir Edward Dempster, whose family lived in the isolated splendour of Houghton Manor. Even before the outbreak of war, Charles Dempster had aimed at a military career or, more accurately as a second son, been aimed at it. The Nicholson family only knew the Dempsters from their grace and favour visits to the village for fetes or church services. Charles was a formidable, muscular man by his twenties, good-looking in a severe, dark way, generally expressionless beyond a vaguely malevolent frown and with a brooding presence which hinted at suppressed violence. The village children kept out of his way.

So the sensation when he appeared, in 1938, with the metropolitan Sadie on his arm, whose smooth, colourful clothes ('silk; she's wearing silk,' Alan's mother breathed incredulously), and pallor of complexion set her far apart from the simple attire and ruddy country glow of the local women. People then travelled rarely; when Dempster had gone to London for military training, he had rapidly faded from memory. And here he was, in glorious full dress uniform and even, unbelievably, smiling in a way that showed white teeth and robust good health. The village people watched silently as the Dempsters and their noble associates swept in and out of the church, entranced by the wild extravagance of it all - abundant flowers, expensive shining vehicles, men morning-suited, women with startling hats, and even in such company, Sadie looking radiantly beautiful, so much so that Alan's father glanced at the women around him and whispered to him, 'you can almost hear their teeth grinding,' followed by that mischievous grin of his. Alan grinned back happily without understanding a word; he was nine years old.

'She does look wonderful,' Alan's mother said, as if conceding an argument. 'Quite, quite stunning.'

One particular characteristic of Sadie's, for all that, communicated itself to Alan, child as he was. Faultless as everything seemed to be, a nervousness, a hint of jittery self-deprecation, lived in those big, soft brown eyes, which blinked frequently and sometimes darted about as if unsure of her company. And, as she hung on Dempster's arm, the great gleaming hulk of him did make her seem so vulnerable by comparison, even though her voice, with its strange, grating accent, could always be heard distinctly from a distance.

They moved into that hybrid house by the river, a modest enough home compared to the Manor, but Dempster's brusque, down to earth soldier had rather detached him from his parents' pseudo-aristocratic pretensions. The house had stood empty for years and the local boys had commandeered the land around, all the way down to the banks either side of the river, for fishing, mucking about, and occasionally, in summer, skinny dipping. Soon, the spot was largely abandoned, especially the skinny dipping, since the riverbanks could be seen from the house and everyone knew who was master of it.

Then, of course, September 1939 and war; Dempster left and was rarely seen again. Sadie found herself alone in the house with two old family retainers. She tried to throw herself into local life, with coffee mornings or help with war efforts to raise money, clothes or food, but the local women continued to distrust her. By 1941, the rumours had started, so salacious that Alan's mother wouldn't allow them to be repeated in the house. Sadie Dempster, it was said, was 'taking in men,' which, to the local children, meant lodgers, but everyone knew Sadie, being a Dempster, could not possibly be short of money,

109

so speculation moved into areas where the children were out of our depth, vaguely connected with the slop of kisses and such and too soppy for the boys in particular to bother themselves about.

But, of course, they were growing up, and the older they got, the more fascinating the slop became. Then, in May 1943, a message arrived at the village post office for immediate delivery to the Dempster house by the river. By then, everyone knew exactly what those messages looked like. Dempster's remains came back a week later and the funeral took place, to Alan's young mind grotesquely, in the same church where the marriage had been celebrated five years before. The toll taken on Sadie was clear enough; she was dressed in mourning, much like the other women, but still set apart from them by her remaining pallor, that peculiar voice, and still those darting eyes moving even more desperately in her distress. Her brother appeared with her at the funeral, displaying evident animosity towards the local people. For the first time, everyone found out that Sadie's maiden name was Denham, though few of them were interested enough to care.

At fourteen, Alan's growing impatience with the village was fuelled by his indignation at the subsequent treatment of Sadie Dempster, left alone in her big house by the river and apparently branded as disreputable without any cause or evidence visible to him. He got short shrift whenever he asked about it.

'Not your business, Alan,' his mother would say, her eyes hardening, 'and hopefully never will be.'

By one September evening in 1944, when fifteen-year-old Alan set off with John Mitchell to find something to do with themselves, his life was changing fast. Most boys had left school, including John, and the only reason Alan hadn't was his parents' insistence that he should continue at school and get the Higher School Certificate. Colleges and universities were being talked about, and in any case, the desire was growing rapidly within him to get away and see what the rest of the world had to offer. The village community began to feel like a brake on his life.

No-one went near the Dempster place any more, mainly because boys were forbidden by their parents, backed up with threats of the painful repercussions which were common enough then. The absence of others was the main reason why John and Alan went there, to temporarily free John from persecution. John, again unfairly from Alan's justice-centred young mind, was picked on because of his father. Walter Mitchell, still of military age, had no apparent physical or health problems apart from some supposed back trouble, but he had never been called up. He was a big, lumbering man, who moved awkwardly enough to suggest a grain of truth in the back story, and little was ever said to his face; his capacity for violence was well known, back or no back. Most of the time he was amiable enough, with a great shock of curly hair and odd, cold blue eyes, but the menace was there, even in the smile. John and Alan used to smoke – almost every boy did then, because their fathers did - in the outhouses of the Mitchell place, and Mitchell caught them red-handed once, when they were both twelve.

The boys had assumed they were safe amongst the innumerable boxes and stacks; he suddenly popped up behind them almost as if he'd been waiting. Knowing that he would have no case to defend even if he was prepared to go crying to his mother, which he wasn't, Alan had no choice but to take the same medicine as John. Mitchell thrashed both boys with his belt, one at a time, across his knees, on and on until they were raw and whimpering. Even by the harsh standards of the time, it

111

was cruel and degrading punishment, and Mitchell's apparent relish in inflicting it, even on his own son, marked him down in Alan's mind as a deeply unpleasant and somewhat unbalanced man.

The friends made themselves cleverer after that, and he never caught them together again, though they suspected that he'd tried. However, while Alan could avoid him, John couldn't, and when John had clearly been beaten again, Alan supported him largely by pretending not to notice his glumness and even staying with him when he cried, an alarming experience between boys.

It had become obvious to everyone in the village that Mitchell was a black market dealer, peddling goods, including foods, which were either unavailable or severely rationed. The people who knew included, of course, the boy population. Mitchell himself being too tough to handle, the boys did as boys do and went for the easier target, John, tall but lean, with the snaking, uncoordinated limbs of adolescence. He never lacked courage, which meant he retained the grudging respect of some, but he took things to heart and smiled very little. Fathers became a taboo subject between the friends. Alan's was out in the Atlantic in a particularly vicious and uncomfortable scenario of war clear enough from the newsreels, and Alan missed him with a physical, endless ache, like a stitch. John's pained him in more immediate and literal ways; for both friends, the exposed wounds stayed untouched as much as possible.

But escape from the public eye wasn't the only reason why the boys were there that night, even though neither of them could have articulated it. The idea of knowing more about the 'slop' legends around Sadie Dempster tempted both of them. They were teenage boys; they needed to get up to a few stupid pranks, mess about

112

sometimes, and even more so in the middle of a war which seemed to them to have been going on for an eternity and which meant they were often surrounded by unhappy or anxious people. 'Slop,' which wasn't interesting, was also turning into sex, which was, and Sadie did seem connected with the whole mysterious but increasingly fascinating business. They both knew boys who said they had had experiences with girls which neither of them could honestly claim to have had. Even though they knew much of it was just talk, the notion that they were missing out on something very adult festered inside them.

Every boy in the village had sometimes used tree climbing to look into what they were not supposed to see. John and Alan were expert tree climbers by then, swift and total disappearance being necessary on occasions. And there did seem to be an awful lot of very large trees in those days.

The night was drawing in as the friends heard a group of boys coming closer around the bend in the river. They could make out each of the four voices, and none of them were friends.

At the top of the bank, next to the Dempster house, was a giant oak tree, its outline huge and menacing in the gloom. Though Alan and John had never yet done it themselves, boys said that the upper branches provided views right into the Dempster house, and the temptation to kill both the birds of escape and investigation was just too good to miss.

'It'll have to be the Dempster tree, John,' Alan said. 'There's just nothing else for it.'

By the time the gang below were where the friends had been, Alan and John had reached the upper branches of the tree, and they could see who was below, two of them being the Simmons brothers, and Mick, the seventeen year old older one, would probably have been a handful for John and Alan on his own. What all of them could have done to the friends, next to water and in near-darkness, didn't bear thinking about.

And they simply would not go away. Alan and John sat there, not daring to move and consequently getting colder, while the boys below fooled around, chucking stones into the water and kicking a ball about. Maybe they were also hooked on the Sadie legends. By the time they eventually drifted off, the friends were numb, but they'd noticed that the night was now full-mooned.

They needed to stay hidden for a little longer, and they edged across to the branches nearest the house. The temptation to gain some kind of benefit, however dubious, from this inglorious incident was just too much. The full moon made the house luminous, outlined against the night sky.

And there they saw, through a large, uncurtained window, a naked man on top of a naked woman, the actual thing they now vaguely knew adults did to make babies and for the salacious pleasure of it. It seemed an untidy, undignified affair, the man's enormous behind rising and falling and the woman, Sadie without a doubt, being pounded on as if she was an inanimate object. They felt frightened for her, with her flushed cheeks and moist, wild eyes. Eventually, the man arched backwards and cried out clearly enough for the boys to hear him. Sadie's mouth opened even wider, looking like a desperate silent cry for help. The man sat up beside the bed and picked up a packet of cigarettes. Having lit one, he stood up and moved towards the window. Alan's chest twisted and his breath caught in his throat; the man was, quite unmistakably, John's father.

Alan looked across at John, whose long body was stretched along a strong bough, with his hands holding

114

on to two branches. His eyes flickered back and no words were said, but they'd known each other since babyhood and Alan could easily see that John had recognised his father some time ago, because his set jaw and thin mouth were reactions, not surprise. His glazing eyes and pale knuckles were indications of suspicions confirmed. Alan had forgotten or dismissed the rumours about Sadie and Mitchell; for John, of course, such indifference was impossible.

Within days, that night by the river became a pushed domino setting off an irrevocable chain reaction, and Alan's life became a sequence of departures.

Firstly, John ran away. In those war days, when communications were so difficult, disappearing from somewhere was quite easily achieved. He came to Alan's place three days after the nocturnal experience and they talked in a secluded part of the garden.

'I have to go, Alan,' John said. 'I can't stand this any longer. Being persecuted on his behalf was just about tolerable when I had some belief in him, but that has gone now. I have to go.'

Alan saw his friend had a pack on his back; he really did mean 'go.' For over an hour Alan tried to talk him out of it, but he knew he ultimately had little more to offer than platitudes about time healing, and John just sat there shaking his head and half-smiling, in a kind of fatalistic melancholy.

'Alright, alright,' Alan said at last. 'If you must. But take something from me; you can't leave the village with nothing but hate, John.'

Alan went to his room and got his scout knife, once his pride and joy but now fading into boyhood, with its ivory handle and scout association insignia. He also took a little money he'd saved from holiday and odd jobs. As he came down the stairs to the back door, he was

115

suddenly afraid that John had already gone, but he was there, hovering between sitting and standing, thin and awkward. He protested, until Alan cut him off in mid-sentence.

'This is the price of my co-operation, John. Taking these things is what it costs.'

John put the knife and the money in his coat and when he lifted his head, his whole face was unashamedly awash with tears. They shook hands, which was all boys could do in those days, and John just turned and walked away.

Next to go was Sadie Dempster, belatedly rescued by her own family, the Denhams, whose own war in London had been traumatic enough to fully occupy them. The local tongues wagged more viciously than ever about her and Mitchell, though neither of the boys ever said anything about that night to anyone.

Sadie left only weeks after the war in Europe ended. Without John, Alan could move about without threat of abuse, verbal or otherwise, but after having experienced such local viciousness, Alan only really trusted his own company. He saw a car parked across the street from Mitchell's warehouse, where Mitchell and two of his men were unloading some goods. Alan recognised the person in the passenger seat as Sadie, looking gaunt and unwell, the eyes still flickering around. The driver was her brother, Simon Denham, who Alan remembered from Dempster's funeral, a lean, angry-eyed man who looked capable of quick, violent action at a moment's notice. There were growing numbers of such men around after the war, demobbed soldiers who'd lived with danger for years and had become quite dangerous themselves.

Denham moved determinedly across the street towards Mitchell. Mitchell's men tried to carry on as if nothing was happening, and so, at first, did Mitchell

116

himself, lumbering boxes in and out with that usual odd slightly limping gait. Denham stopped some twenty yards away and called Mitchell's name, attaching a few words which Mitchell could not ignore.

Then and there, Denham said his piece, and though Alan was too far away to make out every word – Denham's voice was a hoarse growl – it was clear enough that what he said amounted to a very pointed threat concerning what would happen if their paths should ever cross again. I think the only reason he didn't set about Mitchell was because Sadie had asked him not to. In the car, she became agitated, twisting a handkerchief around in her hands and glancing around as if she expected a policeman to arrive. Mitchell's men had very pointedly wandered away. Denham made one final and very emphatic gesture which I was now old enough to understand, and strode back to his car.

Sadie was clearly leaving the village for good. For some reason, perhaps because of Alan's resentment at the way the village had judged and condemned her, he didn't want her to go without some faint kindness from someone. He rode his bike quickly to Sadie's car window and tapped on it, immediately flinching away from Denham's murderous stare and concentrating on Sadie's pools of hazel eyes, even more affecting at close quarters.

'You don't know me, Mrs. Dempster, I'm just one of the local kids. But not everyone in this village thinks badly of you. Good luck, whatever you do.'

I held out my hand. Denham's stare became something vaguely like a smile. Rather than take Alan's hand, Sadie reached out and bent his head towards her, kissing one cheek and then the other, while he felt them both burn.

'I know you, Alan, and thank you. Good luck to you too, though I doubt a boy as clever as you will need it.'

117

The car chugged off and Alan stayed frozen to the spot, completely blown away by the kisses and the revelation of someone who hardly knew him perceiving him as 'clever.' It did help a boy from a country village to summon up enough confidence to get out into the world.

The next and infinitely more welcome departure was Mitchell's. Through the last months of 1945 and into 1946, Mitchell's war gradually emerged into the light. Sadie's case was a variant on a number of similar situations. Left almost entirely to her own devices by the Dempsters after the death of Charles and inheriting only the house and a war widow's pension, Sadie needed help to keep the two servants who were her only company, and Mitchell provided it – at a price. Most other Mitchell cases were also widows, but some were the wives of returning soldiers or men missing presumed dead who had reappeared. The women were simply seeking to provide decently for their families in the teeth of severe rationing and absent husbands. Mitchell preyed on them, beginning with a few off ration morsels and moving onto black market goods and money loans. What became apparent in time was that only Mitchell had ever been granted sexual favours at the Dempster house, but her activities with him were enough to spread the rumours, actively supported by women seeking to deflect suspicion from themselves.

By late 1946, life for Mitchell was getting very precarious indeed. Returning men pieced together information from various sources. One November night, the misguided loyalty of an ex-supplier of Mitchell warned him that a gang of village men intended to do him severe damage. That same night, he and his wife Jean packed the large Jaguar boot with all they could and sped out of the village, not without a well-aimed stone shattering the rear window of their car. He employed

118

men to come back a few weeks later and clear the remains of the Mitchell place before it went on the market, though by that time it had been widely looted and the local constabulary didn't seem inclined to do very much about it.

The penultimate departure was Alan's, not long after the dreadful winter of 1947 had finally subsided. His success in the Higher School Certificate meant that even his mother conceded that to do what he hoped to do in life meant leaving the small world of the village. He left for a town big enough to have a newspaper of its own, and in time, having made enough tea and run enough errands to start climbing the journalistic slippery pole, he moved up to the metropolis itself and found opportunity enough to explore just how big the world was outside that little village.

He never heard of Sadie Dempster again; she didn't return to the village and presumably found another life back with her own family. Alan never saw or heard from John Mitchell again either, but he suspected in the years immediately after John left he was afraid of post being intercepted, and after that the village represented such an unhappy, even dangerous, time of his life that he totally disassociated himself from it mentally as well as physically. Mitchell himself was arrested in 1948, charged with a whole catalogue of crimes relating to black marketeering and extortion, with a huge battery of willing witnesses against him, and imprisoned.

The fourth, last and saddest departure was not from a place, or a time. It was from a life, and the life was that of my father, the boy in this story, Alan Nicholson. He died at the age of eighty-six in his retirement apartment in 2015. There had been talk of moving him into a hospice, but his condition was such – I won't particularise – that it was accepted he would do as well to stay in what he had left of a home. After my mother's death in 2010, I made what attempts I could to plug at least some of the gigantic chasm that her death had opened up in his life and hold together the rent it had made in mine.

I am an only child; my mother's health problems didn't start in later life, unfortunately, and her health was the shadow that had hung over the three of us all of my life, while we all, especially her, did our best to shoo it away with a studied amiability between us. As Alan himself began to fade in late 2013, I visited him as often as I could, with other commitments such as my own children and grandchildren restricting time and opportunity. When it became clear that his time was very limited, my wife Kate and I worked at organising our time so I could go to Dad at least once every two days.

Such a frequency of visits made it difficult not to go over the same conversational ground, even though there were times when I could do little more than watch him sleep. I tried to talk about Mum as much as I could; it pained him when people felt it was an unmentionable subject, as those around him sometimes seemed to do. However, as we approached the end, many of the memories of Mum were beginning to upset him, and I felt we needed, occasionally at least, to find other things to talk about, which would keep us on less demanding ground as his strength ebbed away. And yes, there was an element of selfishness involved. Losing him, as I was clearly about to do, so soon after losing her, even allowing for their ages, was a hammer blow to me, and for me to start getting distressed and tearful in his presence was hardly likely to make anything better.

'I've never known much about your life before Mum, Dad,' I said. 'I can't remember you ever saying much about your younger years, for example. You were born not far from here, weren't you?'

He was on one of his better days, when he had enough breath available, and it soon became clear that I had unlocked a box kept hidden away for a long time.

'Yes, I was, Peter. Leaving the village was the first big departure of my life, and like others to follow, it taught me a lot. With the final departure approaching – no, it's alright, Peter, I'm coming to terms with it in my own way – it makes sense for me to tell you something of the first.'

What he told me then is the story I have told now. I became the only person who had ever heard it; he considered it too risqué in parts to even tell my mother.

For me, it acts as a tribute and a memorial to him, a man whose innate decency and civilisation was even apparent in boyhood and adolescence, those wildest of times.

He died shortly after the seventieth anniversary of the end of World War II, and his story throws a light on the women and children of the war and the toll it took on people away from the main theatres of fighting. Yes, every generation has to deal with personal arrivals and departures, but I, as a child and teenager, didn't have to deal with my father away fighting in the Atlantic and knowing that each and every day could see him killed or mutilated. I didn't have to grow up in a community suddenly deprived of fathers, and prey to the evil, self-interested men who contrived a way out of being in the forces.

When he died, I found he still had some letters he exchanged with his father during the war. His father's prose is very gung-ho and a little awkward; Dad always reckoned most of his writing ability came from his mother, born into a generation, of course, when women's career opportunities were rather more limited than they are now. His own writing, doing his level best to conceal the anguished son in tales of school triumphs and

121

domestic peace, reduced me to tears and I say that with a lot of pride and no shame.

NEW DAY AT NETHER BARTON

Cavendish Grange had been the pride and joy of Nether Barton for generations. Built originally as a home on the land given by a grateful Henry VII to one of his stalwart supporters, a professional soldier called Richard Cavendish, after the unlikely triumph of the Battle of Bosworth in 1485, it gradually developed as the Cavendish family continued to prosper through the reigns of five Tudor monarchs. As the main Cavendish criterion for deciding their political and religious beliefs was which ones were identified with the winning side, they also saw their way relatively unscathed through the English Civil War and the subsequent Stuart dynasty as well.

By the time of the Hanoverian succession, the family's facility for jumping the right way continued when another soldier, William Cavendish, served with distinction under the Duke of Marlborough in his battles with the armies of Louis XIV. His reward was to be made a hereditary baronet by Queen Anne, and further additions to the extensive if disjointed family seat followed.

William becoming Sir William and able to pass the 'sir' on to his male heirs sealed the Cavendish pre-eminence in their area of rural Buckinghamshire, but their fortunes rose and fell with Big Dipper-like irregularity through the industrial revolutions and the two world wars. Finally, the death of Sir George Cavendish in 2005 and his wife Elizabeth in 2008 sealed the fate of the Grange.

The actual number of children sired by Sir George had been an interesting local conjecture for some time, before and after he became Sir George in 1975, but unfortunately only one of them was legitimate. This was the redoubtable Cecilia Cavendish, whose typical reaction to pleas directed at her to 'save the family line' usually included three assertions; one, she was not a 'breed mare' and had no intention of becoming one, two, the Cavendishes were 'a worthless bunch of so-and-sos who were better off extinct,' and three, 'no-one can afford to run this bloody barn of a house now anyway.'

Predictably enough in view of number three, Cecilia nevertheless shocked the family and neighbourhood by selling the entire house and estate in 2012 and retreating to comfortable exile in Provence.

Cavendish Grange then underwent a period of hiatus. The local rumour that the National Trust had acquired the house was scotched by the Trust itself, and it emerged eventually that the Grange had been bought by a consortium intending to establish a private school for the performing arts. This was not generally well-received either by the council's Planning Committee or the local community. Speculation about the 'kind of people' who would now be inhabiting the Grange and 'whether such an establishment is viable in our community' filled the letters pages of local papers.

When it became clear that the consortium's plans included the demolition of parts of the Grange and the selling-off of local land currently still with long-standing tenancies, the Council made clear that planning permission would not be forthcoming unless substantial changes were made. The battle continued to and fro for four years, with the local people for once largely on the Council's side, until in 2016 several members of the consortium withdrew their interest and the project effectively disintegrated.

Placed in the hands of agents who seemed unable to arouse much interest, the Grange spent two years slowly crumbling towards dereliction, to the outrage of the community. No-one appeared to have sufficient resources or motivation to rescue the house, and as the damage grew more visible, several local politicians put together a consortium of their own, though only to repair and maintain the building, not modernise it or give it new purpose.

In the spring of 2018, it was announced that permission had been properly sought and obtained to turn the Grange into a luxury hotel. Rumours that some of those charged with granting permissions had been 'bought' by the Corporation concerned were rife, but nothing could be proved, and generally speaking, supporters outnumbered opponents throughout the local area. At least, people thought, the Grange would be 'done up properly,' to attract 'the better sort' of tourists and give a boost to local employment.

However, the new owners remained a mystery. They had been named as the Markham Corporation, a company with 'widespread interests in the leisure and tourism sectors,' and concern grew as Nether Bartonians were made aware through the local press that Markham interests included several 'leisure parks' which one local councillor described as 'little better than caravan sites.' Bert Meadows, well-respected landlord and owner of the Cavendish Arms, which offered bed and breakfast rooms, spoke for many when he said 'if it's to be theme parks, bouncy castles, or noisy pop concerts, we'd much sooner Markham, whoever they are, took their business elsewhere.'

Nevertheless, when the Markham Corporation opened up job applications to local people,

they rapidly had at least four or five applicants for each post, including one from Bert's chief barmaid Bev Shaw, who explained to the landlord that she was 'looking to move up in the world, and I think I'm worth it, Mr. Meadows.'

Reassurance grew throughout the rest of 2018 as the extent of the Grange's refurbishment became apparent. Anxiety about the demolition of the stables and other outhouses were eased when it was realised that they were to be rebuilt as holiday apartments surrounding the main buildings. When a large barn started being converted to an indoor swimming pool with saunas and hot tubs, Nether Barton began to find itself substantially pleased with its plush new acquisition.

However, the signposts announcing the opening of the hotel in 2019 bemused many people. Expectations of the 'Cavendish Grange Hotel,' or even just 'The Grange,' were dashed when the name was announced as the 'Markham Arms Hotel,' with an unrecognised coat of arms featuring prominently on the sign.

Saturday May 18th 2019 was chosen for the Grand Opening, and those local people already in post as hotel staff were well pleased with the standard of the equipment, décor and accommodation. Melanie Rowan of the cleaning staff breathlessly told her friends in the Clock Tea Rooms 'it's 'top end.' They've spared no expense and make a really nice job of it.'

The 'top end' approach extended to the staff as well. The Head Chef, it seemed, had been lured away from his London base with the offer of a very fine salary. The General Manager, Peter Karelski, a Pole, was another recruit from London, and formerly assistant manager of a large hotel in Mayfair. The cleaning and housekeeping staff supervisor was an Asian lady called Kashvi Prasanna, head-hunted from a similar post in a large hotel in Birmingham. The grumblers who complained that no locals had been allowed to take the top jobs had it gently pointed out to them that none of the population of

126

Nether Barton could be said to have the right qualifications.

As the big launch day approached, supporters and opponents were about evenly divided. Bert Meadows at the Cavendish Arms, as ever, spoke for the latter.

'Well, I don't know exactly what or who it's for, but it isn't for us, that's for sure.'

Some of his customers nodded, but they noticeably didn't include the butcher, the baker and three local farmers, who knew their contracts with the Markham Arms would keep them securely in business for some time.

One solitary resident spotted what she thought was a local connection. The retired headteacher of Nether Barton Primary School, Edith Williams, now in her early nineties, musing in the Tea Rooms, said 'Markham sounds like the surname of a young woman who lived here for a while, a long time ago now.' Mrs. Williams' mental archive of local people was legendary, but on this occasion, she seemed to be alone in her recollection and some wondered whether dear Mrs. Williams was finally drifting into her dotage.

Wednesday May 15th 2019, 18.37, Nether Barton Station

Trains passed through Nether Barton on their way to and from the metropolis frequently, but only two a day actually stopped, at 08.30 to London and 18.25 from it. The timetabled times were not always accurate, and on this occasion, the lag was twelve minutes. Nether Barton's little band of commuters, today numbering four, were emerging before the train actually stopped and they then moved rapidly towards the station exits, as if determined to start reclaiming their twelve minutes immediately.

Only when the train had firmly stopped did a fifth figure descend in a more sedate fashion. He was a very well-dressed and clean shaven man, with piercing, alert grey eyes, a brisk manner and an authoritative way of walking, as if used to being listened to and obeyed. The random streaks of grey in his temples hinted at a greater age than other clues suggested. He was not particularly tall, in the region of five feet ten inches, but his broad, square shoulders and powerful legs suggested that his way of earning his living had not always been as genteel as his made to measure suit and clean grooming implied.

He carried no luggage, and after a few determined strides along the platform, he found himself pausing, perhaps to get his bearings, but more like a man returning to a place he had known long ago. As, indeed, he was.

Robert Lethbridge, Chief Executive and majority shareholder of Markham Corporation, detected a scent, an amalgamation of nice and nasty rural aromas suddenly evocative of his distant childhood. The last time he had stood on this platform he had been eight years old, full fifty years ago. The station's immensity and cloak of mystery and promise, all-consuming as it was then, was now so absolutely a thing of distant childhood that something generally unfamiliar to him, a scintilla of doubt about his actions, stopped him in his tracks. He knew well enough where and what London was now; he had had no concept of it then other than a huge menacing leviathan, which could either be the setting for endless elaborate, challenging games or a monster intent on consuming him and his lonely, preoccupied mother in one predatory bite.

He gazed across the line to the platform on the London-bound side, and he could almost see again his mother standing there in her shabby brown coat,

128

patiently if testily fending off his questions, with her right hand in his and her left wrenching nervously at the handkerchief in her pocket. He'd been frightened enough, about to leave everything he'd ever known, but her whole bearing intensified his fear. She came from London, but she was only going back because she felt she had to, and what kind of place was it which induced such distress at the prospect of returning to it? He was only eight, but he wasn't blind or stupid, and he'd never seen her like this; she was a brave, competent and organised woman, who lived her life and went her own way, whatever anyone thought about it.

'Let you run about with London boys? No fear, Bobby. You'd be like my brothers, getting up to all sorts. You're better off growing up here, believe me.'

His memory of this speech was shaky – he can't have been older than five or six, but the gist of it went home well enough. And now here she was, standing on the platform ready to take both of them back to 'the Smoke,' as she called it, conjuring up in his mind a huge, dark place where all sorts of evil deeds took place without people being able to see them.

He knew the journey from the village to the Station well enough. The first time he'd ever actually been on a train was that final exit to London, but trains and exits fascinated him from an early age, and simply seeing the trains fly by, or heave to a halt with such magnificent cacophonies of noise, made the half mile or so from his house worth the trip.

Very occasionally, he'd had a companion, but never companions. He remembered how demeaning he'd found it then, the reluctance of so many other children to have anything to do with him, and his endless reviews of the various things which might be wrong with him – did he smell? Well, he washed as regularly as any others – better than some of them, who did smell. Was he too loud, boring, stupid? Orgies of self-examination throughout the innocence of childhood were among the scores he had to settle with Nether Barton. He knew now why so many kids had steered clear of him, and the fact that it did neither them nor their parents much credit didn't change the reality of what had happened.

His new hotel was on the other side of Nether Barton, meaning he would have to walk through the village to get to it. He'd thought about asking Peter Karelski to send someone to pick him up but, as General Manager, Karelski would be up to his eyes in work now. It had partly been Karelski who'd encouraged him into the hotel venture. Though the man was fifteen years his junior, their life connections including childhoods both subjected to bigotry which they'd explored on a slightly inebriated night in Mayfair. However, much as he identified with Karelski's struggles as a young immigrant's son in East London, it was the superb way he ran his hotel which brought about their professional association. The morepies the Markham Corporation plunged its fingers into, the more its C.E. sought out people already well acquainted with each and every pie.

He noted the curious looks, though none of them, he could see, were of recognition. Not many people wandered through Nether Barton in the early evening in a Savile Row suit. It immediately put a barrier between him and them, allowing him the chance to recall if he wished and reject if he didn't.

By the general store, he paused. It was still open, and appeared now to be an off licence as well. Of course, the décor and window were all different, but the family name was still there. How many times he had stood next to the counter here, his face only just about peeping over it, and looked up at old Marjorie Mellors. The best he ever got from her was a curled lip, a face flinched away as if he was an evil smell below her oddly flared nostrils, and something along the lines of 'what do you want, boy? Tell me quickly and then off you go.'

Old Marjorie Mellors, he assumed, was long gone, but it seemed the Mellors were not. One of them, Alan Mellors, had been one of his serial young tormentors, boys smaller than him who attempted to provoke him into violence against them so that more general retribution could be visited on him by their older friends or brothers. And he knew as soon as he walked in that the man standing behind the counter was Alan Mellors. For a while, the two men's eyes met, and Robert saw clearly enough Alan's resemblance to old Marjorie. The face contorting itself into what was presumably supposed to be a welcoming smile looked just as given to curled lips and a sneering mouth.

The silence reached awkward lengths.

'Can I help you?' Mellors said at last, and even the voice, Robert thought, had the same thin, put upon quaver as Marjorie's.

'Will you be attending the hotel opening, Mr. Mellors?' Robert said. The other man again duplicated, almost exactly, his mother's disgusted flinch.

'I don't think we've ever met, have we? Is that your business, whoever you are?'

Robert moved towards the counter. Mellors noticed the build, the eyes and the expensive suit. He paled and his eyebrows dropped into question and doubt.

'Yes, we've met, Alan,' Robert said, placing his hands apart on the counter. 'A long time ago. Do come to the opening, Alan. Such a prestigious local event. You might just enhance your local history. Local history is very important, isn't it?'

131

He smiled, even as his eyes narrowed. Mellors paled and backed further away. Robert turned and walked out. Was that what he intended, he thought? Whether or not, it was probably an effective idea. If Alan Mellors resembled his gossipy mother, and he suspected he did, this incident would be all over the village by this time tomorrow. He would certainly have a generous turn out of locals at the opening now. And, in any case, encountering one of the Mellors family as a big, grown man had given him a very definite vicarious satisfaction

But, just in case, he decided on another short detour to the local garage, only another fifty yards up the road. This time, the old family name, Castleton, had disappeared, and the only name on display was the neutral 'Auto Centre,' rather irregularly emblazoned over the premises; large banner letters here, small print with an odd van-like design there.

A car was way beyond the reach of his mother, though it could have saved her many exhausting hours trudging to and from her work. Perhaps because of their simple unavailability, however, cars fascinated him, and for a while as a seven year old he would hang about the garage and talk to the men, some of them not much more than boys, who worked on the Castleton premises.

They were generally cheerful fellows, if enmeshed in oil and grease, and willing enough to discuss the motors they had in and what they were doing to them. For a few weeks, he would turn up and they seemed to start seeing him as a kind of mascot. Sometimes, they would even let him crawl under the car they were servicing and explain to him what they were doing.

The standing joke was the car he was going to buy his mother when he was old enough, and some of the men even laughingly argued with each other about which would best suit 'little Bob's lady mother,' and put their case to him as he was a new customer on the forecourt about to buy the car that very day.

Everything continued amicably enough, until the day when Castleton himself was in residence. Robert knew from what the men had said that Mr. Castleton was largely an absentee owner, and they also said other things, sweary things that he didn't understand, about the owner, though they usually said them when they thought he couldn't hear.

He was talking to Rory, one of the younger lads, when Castleton appeared in person, a well-built, dark man, his expression seemingly set firmly in a scowl.

'What's 'e doing here?' Castleton demanded of Rory, who couldn't find an answer.

'Bugger off, you. Don't want your sort round here,' Castleton growled, and then, turning to Rory, 'if you don't want to collect your cards, son, you'd better concentrate on what you're paid for. Never mind chatting with kids, and especially not that one.'

Robert began to slink away, but not before he'd looked at Castleton's features long and carefully, and vowed to himself, 'I'll come back for you, my fine friend, when I'm big enough.' Then he ran to one of his favourite and most private trees, climbed up into the thickest branches, and wept quietly until some of the pain ebbed away.

Returning to the present like an awakening, he saw a youngish man with a friendly face striding towards him. He realised he must have been standing and staring into the garage for some minutes.

'Can I help you, sir?' the man said.

'Oh, I'm just remembering,' he said. 'The last time I stood here, I was eight years old. It had the name Castleton all over it.'

'Oh, yes, of course. Goodness, that's going back a bit.'

Robert looked again at the healthy young face, and an unfamiliar wave of embarrassment swept over him.

'Memories, memories,' he said vaguely. 'Well, must get on.'

He resumed his walk, wondering why and how something so obvious, that a great deal of Nether Barton time had passed since he was last here, could suddenly be such a revelation. Yes, of course, there was an entire generation – two generations – who simply hadn't been born when he and his mother lived here and were therefore guiltless of persecution. It was oddly comforting and reassuring, reminding him that his relationship with this place as it now was did not need to be so acrimonious and full of recrimination. However, what he had planned for the evening would go ahead as planned, for the sake of his late mother.

Saturday May 18th 2019, 15.23, Resolution Lounge, Markham Arms Hotel.

In the 300-capacity elegant if contemporary Resolution Restaurant, the celebratory lunch marking the opening of the hotel was winding to a good-humoured close. The media people, while entertained elsewhere during the lunch, were now re-admitted, and cameras placed in the generous space available all pointed towards the top table. Journalists had researched the twenty top-tablers and had already identified two peers of the realm and several well-known travel writers and commentators.

The hubbub of conversation died down as the General Manager, Peter Karelski, tall, dark and imposing, rose to his feet.

'My lords, ladies and gentlemen,' he said, and the resonation of his voice testified to the superior acoustics of the room. 'As you can see behind me, we have two large blank screens with a pair of beautifully made closed velvet curtains between them. All will, I'm sure, become clear. It gives me great pleasure to introduce to you the Chief Executive of the Markham Corporation, Mr. Robert Lethbridge.'

As well-wined and dined applause crackled around the hall, Edith Williams, centrally placed in a table of local people, suddenly found herself digging another memory gold nugget from the dimness which so oppressed her these days. It couldn't be, she thought, but just perhaps it really was. He was, of course, much older and fuller in the face, and his name was different, but who he resembled most was, to her at least, so embarrassingly obvious that she was amazed no-one had picked up on it. Then she paused to glance around her, and it became clear from a few frozen faces that some probably had.

'My lords, ladies and gentlemen,' Lethbridge started, and the room's acoustics made his public address voice boom to every corner of the lounge. The tinge of London cockney was not pronounced, but evident.

'In the normal course of events, my good lady Anne and other members of my family would be here with me today, but as they all have busy lives of their own, and as my history here doesn't actually connect much with them, we decided I could keep this one for myself and the Company.'

Behind him, on one of the screens, a large face suddenly appeared. It was a black and white photograph of a young woman looking directly and unashamedly into the camera. The size of the image brought alive the intelligence and determination in the clear eyes, complemented by the firm mouth, with the lips slightly parted in an uncertain smile.

'This, ladies and gentlemen, is my mother, the late Ellen, usually known as Ellie, Lethbridge, only in this picture she wasn't called that. At this time, she was known as Ellie Markham.'

An audible gasp rose from the local tables, including a few further flung associates of the Cavendish family. Edith Williams nodded and smiled; the past had yet to desert her.

Robert stopped to gather his thoughts. He had worked on this, in his own mind and with the help of others, for some time, and he was determined not to compromise it now.

'Ellie Markham lived in Nether Barton between 1959 and 1969, quite a decade in her life. She was twenty when she arrived and thirty when she left. She was born in 1939, three months before the outbreak of the Second World War, in Stepney, in the East End of London, and by 1945, she and her brothers Tommy and Ed were orphans. Her father Walter died in the 1944 D-day landings and her mother Beth was killed by a random flying V-bomb only four months before the war ended.

Life in the post-war East End was not easy, and Ellie and her brothers struggled on with the help of uncles, aunts and cousins, and some criminal private enterprise by Tommy and Ed. Then Ellie undertook the kind of work which many working class girls did then; it was called 'going into service.' Even at the age of fourteen, Ellie was seen as a competent, hard-working girl, and a local vicar got her a respectable placing in a house in Ealing.

She became a very junior maid, and even though it meant moving away from her family and everyone she knew, she managed it. She worked for a pleasant enough family called the Moretons, and long as the working days were, she made a good impression. When, in 1959, a more elevated position became available in no less a place than Cavendish Grange, the Moretons even helped her to secure the job.'

A few eyes had dropped on the local tables, and some others, including members of the

Mellor family, were staring fixedly forward, as if trying not to hear. For the moment, utter silence prevailed.

'Now then, so you don't have to just listen to me, let's see another picture, shall we, ladies and gents? Or, even better, another two?'

The faces of two young men appeared beside each other on the other blank screen. This time, the gasp from the local tables was more of a sigh.

'Let me introduce you to these two likely lads. The one on the left is George, not yet Sir George, Cavendish, aged twenty two in 1959. The one on the right is yours truly, aged twenty two in 1983.'

In spite of varying facial expressions and backgrounds, the two young men had a clear and unmistakable resemblance to each other.

'George was a naughty boy, wasn't he, as I think everyone now knows. Ellie wasn't the first or the last young girl to be taken in by George's promises, nor was she the only one to be blanked out by the Cavendish family.'

An elderly man in an old-fashioned suit stamped noisily to his feet and walked away.

'Those who can't stand the heat are entitled to leave the kitchen. Anyone else?'

The silence held, and so did the audience.

'They tried to buy Ellie off with a modest 'gratuity' and an unspoken understanding that she would either leave the area or abort her kid. She did neither; she stayed right there in Nether Barton and she had me, in 1961. Years later, she said to me, 'well, I didn't see that whoever your father was should deprive you of the chance of life. What he did to me was his fault and mine, not yours.'

She said something else to me as well; 'Bobby, I've waited all my life for a home of my own, and now I have one, none of them are going to take it away from me'.'

For the first time, Robert looked overwhelmed. He controlled himself with an effort.

'For eight long years, our little family, mother and son, put up with it. The rumours put around by the Cavendishes that she had a gypsy lover who looked vaguely Cavendish and she was trying her luck. The blank, hostile stares in shops and cafes. One very decent person did support us, and she is with us today, Mrs. Edith Williams, then an innovative young headteacher, who chose to employ Ellie for a few hours a week at the school; Ellie's Moreton family in Ealing included kids, and she was good with kids.

When the outrage of local parents broke over Edith, she used her contacts to get Ellie a position as a nanny eight miles away from Nether Barton, and yes, Ellie would sometimes walk that to go to work. So then the word went round that she was 'going off to see men,' 'working as a prostitute in Buckingham.' No, she was earning an honest and decent living to put bread on the table for her and me.'

He paused, and smiled towards Edith Williams, now wreathed in tears.

'Next time you come here, Mrs. Williams, I hope you will come as my honoured guest. And I promise you it won't be the only occasion.'

His expression immediately changed, as a savage frown swept across it.

'In the summer of 1969, I was set upon by three local kids, and while I gave a decent account of myself – I was a tough little nut by then, I'd had to be - I was still

138

bleeding from several places by the time I got home. My mother had been mulling over a letter from the East End. Her eldest brother Tom had written again. She found those letters from London difficult; she'd had to persuade Tom and Ed not to come to Nether Barton and set about George Cavendish, knowing what the consequences of an assault on the son of the local baronet were likely to be.

Tom and Ed had got over their mad adolescence and teamed up with an uncle and aunt to take over a pub in 1963; they pitched in to the new rock thing and two years later, they had a club as well. By 1969, they were businessmen in the whole concert and catering area, and they wanted Ellie to come back and join them. Determined as she'd always been to make her own way out of the East End, my beating was the main trigger, I think. In spite of her misgivings, we headed back to London.

On Nether Barton station, I remembered her standing there with such an edgy nervousness about whether she was doing the right thing that it got right through to my careless young mind; it wasn't typical of her. She wasn't sure about whether Tom and Ed had made it as well as they said, and though she didn't say so at the time, she thought taking me to grow up in the East End wasn't the best she could do for me.'

Robert paused and looked again at the picture of Ellie. The whole room was still listening, even if there were a few blank stares and lowered heads.

'But, of course, for me it was like all Christmases at once. From just me and Ellie and the good Mrs. Williams, I was suddenly surrounded by uncles, aunts, cousins, even a great uncle and aunt or two. In 1971, Ellie met a young chef called Malc Lethbridge, the guy I've always called Dad, a magic man with permanently amused eyes and a great big heart. She married him before the year

139

was out. Meet my dad Malc, my brother Sam, my sisters June and Sue, and, of course, me and Mum. We never bothered about stepbrothers and stepsisters.'

On one of the screens the whole family appeared, happily close to each other in spite of the age difference between the eighteen year old Robert and the six year old Sue, and they all seemed to be sharing a huge private joke.

'So it should have been the Lethbridge Corporation, shouldn't it? But as the eldest son, the lad who did so much to ensure the business got to be as big as it's become – a lad who doesn't suffer from false modesty – ' – a ripple of quiet laughter relieved the tension in the room – 'I got to decide the final name, and I named it after Ellie. Ellie Markham.'

He stepped over to the curtains covering the big central plaque.

'The coat of arms you are about to see is genuine, and not an invention of mine. Ellie's Markham family also have medieval origins in soldiery, but some prosper, some don't. The winners make the history, yes, but history lasts a long time, and some of the losers can come round again. My lords, ladies and gentlemen, it gives me more pleasure than you can ever imagine to declare open the Markham Arms Hotel, Nether Barton.'

He pulled the cord, and the curtains swished apart to show an ornate crossed sword coat of arms, set above the gold plaque with the words 'Markham Arms Hotel, Nether Barton. Opened by Robert Lethbridge, Chief Executive of the Markham Corporation, Saturday May 18th 2019.'

A growing ripple of applause ran round the room, and Robert noticed Alan Mellors joining in, even if he was clapping as if his hands were on fire. As the cameras exploded in a riot of flash, waiters moved towards the tables carrying champagne bottles. Several minutes later, Robert returned to his position at the top table and began to speak.

'Ladies and gentlemen, I have two toasts to propose. The first one is to Mrs. Edith Williams. This hotel will have a crèche, so that young families can be accommodated, and I hope Mrs. Williams will help us set that up and allow us to name it after her. My lords, ladies and gentlemen, Mrs. Edith Williams!'

As the entire room rose to her, Edith saw again her last sight of Ellie Markham, a quick, moist-eyed glance backwards as she edged her little boy towards the station.

'And finally, we've talked enough of Nether Barton's past, let's look towards its future!

My lords, ladies and gentlemen, here's to the Markham Arms Hotel, Nether Barton!'

Not every toast was enthusiastic, but no-one dissented, and as Edith's eyes settled again on the picture of Ellie, it seemed that a smile had broken across the girl's face. Maybe seeing things in old age, she thought, was really about seeing things other people couldn't see.

THE WAITING CHAIR

June 4th.

Dear Dad,

I came round and shoved this through your door yesterday afternoon when I was on my way to yet another meeting; sitting in meetings seems to be what I spend most of my time doing these days, when I'm not trying to work at home. The lockdown unlocks very slowly; it seems we still can't talk in your house as we used to. We are all thinking of you; I know I've only managed three lockdown letters so far, which isn't very good, but work is very demanding; Council labours are far from dull these days, what with deliveries, advice etc., but family should come first.

I know you're still not too happy with using e-mails and the phone presents hearing problems, but we could perhaps manage something better than waving through windows. Please try to write and let us know how you're coping, as fully as you like; I'll make time and get my priorities right. I'm due to wave at the windows tomorrow; perhaps you could put a letter on the path for me.

I suppose I'm too old now for stories, but you'll remember that many of your stories, which you seemed to be able to make up as you went along, got me writing a few of my own when I was a kid, and took me to new places of the imagination. Letters can help us through this, though hopefully it won't be long before we can meet up; things won't stay as strict as this for very much longer, I'm sure.

And sorry to mention it, but can you reassure me a bit, Dad, please? Dark rumours across the family that your illness is accelerating have got the so-called 'kids,' Sarah and Peter, contacting me on one side, and Jane on the other, with Sarah's husband Dennis now weighing in for good measure. Sarah from abroad, of course, and Jane on home ground, Jane typically wanting the truth, whatever the truth might be. But, of course, it isn't just about alleviating their anxieties, I am anxious myself, and if there's one thing this crisis has taught me, it's that nothing is going to be solved by burying your head in the sand. You used to hold my hand when I was a kid, Dad, when I'd bumped or scratched myself, or yes, I'll admit it now, been fighting with one of those Coulson boys; any chance of me returning the favour?

Your loving son,
Philip

June 5th.

Dear Philip,

What it is to have an athletic neighbour. You perhaps remember little David Cullen, of the Cullens next door, not so little now, and a country standard runner in his spare time. He's allowed out to do his exercise, and he told me yesterday something of his training route when I was standing at the front door getting a bit of air. I realised he was passing your house, so I now have an available postman for our correspondence.

How wonderful to hear from you. Don't castigate yourself too much; I'm not the world's best correspondent myself. You talk about us meeting up quite soon, and I hope so too, very much. I've been thinking back to schooldays recently. Yes, my memory is still that

143

good, at least I think it is, assuming I am remembering what actually happened! It's one subject at least which doesn't connect me to Elaine, and the great chasm in my life her loss has left. But you lost a mother as I lost a wife, and these are not the times or circumstances to dwell on it.

I know we went to the same school, but of course, inevitably, my time was very different from yours; different generations have very varied ways of doing these things. I remembered a particular detail, which was still there in your day because I can remember seeing it when I went there for parents' evening; that chair, which everyone called the waiting chair, outside the headmaster's study. Everybody called them headmasters or headmistresses in those days. Boys – they were all boys at that school then - who were sitting there were usually either going to be beaten or given a pat on the back; unhappily, it was probably more often the former than the latter. Beating children, particularly with the sadistic relish practised by Mr. J.P. Reynolds, M.A., has long since been outlawed, and rightly so; it was hardly surprising that some boys sat there pale and drawn as if about to mount the steps of the guillotine.

But most of us, the normal neither virtuously blameless nor hopelessly criminal majority, were often not too sure, on that chair, whether they were to be punished or praised; such are the ambiguities of boyhood and conscience. I found myself on that chair three times. The first time, I was summoned from a lesson, and I sat trying desperately to work out what was going on and not allow my fear to show. On the plus side, I had just made my debut for the school's under-15 rugby team, and important as that was to me, I couldn't see it concerning such an elevated personage as the Headmaster. On the minus side, I had various minor boyhood sins on my conscience, as about every boy does; at least, I hoped they were minor, while retaining a nasty suspicion that perhaps one or two of them weren't so minor, if seen from the Head's point of view. Even if you weren't actually caught red-handed for some misdemeanour, like smoking in the toilets, which almost everyone did then, there were, then and no doubt now, informers who would snitch – grass you up, is the modern expression. I had been caned once, if somewhat half-heartedly, by a young teacher who thought he needed to throw his weight around and hadn't quite worked out how to identify the habitual villains.

But I'd never had the full Reynolds treatment. It's difficult to convey to people now the mores of over sixty years ago. Beating children; does that mean they were all perverts or unspeakable savages? Well, maybe Reynolds might come into one or both of those categories, yes, but generally speaking, no, it doesn't, it means values have changed, and that isn't just an abstruse historical matter, a footnote in the text books, because people like me lived through it, and are here to tell the tale.

As it turned out, the Head told me that my grandfather was seriously ill and my father was coming to take me to the hospital; my mother, a linguist, as you know, especially since Sarah has inherited the ability, was making her way home from abroad. You never knew my father's father, but I loved him dearly; he was generous, funny and liked to keep a menagerie of animals in his sprawling country home. After all this time, I think I can also fairly say that he had more time for me than my father, quite literally; my parents worked long hours to keep their five children content and prospering, and part of the result was not seeing very much of them.

As we waited for my father, Reynolds was surprisingly solicitous and gentle, in that curious –

curious to us boys, at least - way adults seemed to have of changing manners and attitudes like clothes. I suppose it was only about ten minutes before my father arrived, but it seemed like an eternity. Like most boys, I was genuinely frightened of Reynolds and suspicious of his motives.

As it turned out, Grandpa had had a severe heart attack. For all his virtues, which were many, as far as I was concerned, he never did take proper care of himself. He died only about five minutes after we got to the hospital. But, sitting with my father, the pair of us glum and shattered in a bare hospital side room, I remember very clearly thinking that even an uncompromising Mr. J. P. Reynolds M.A. beating would have been preferable to this.

Of course, I suppose tempting fate with such a thought could only have one result, and the next time I sat on the waiting chair, a beating followed, one which ruled out me sitting on any chairs for some time afterwards. Losing Grandpa sent me off the rails for a while; the adult who had always had the most time and tolerance for me had gone, and I was cast adrift, I suppose; Sam Anderson the bad lad phase set in. I can't remember now the exact sin which provoked the punishment, but there was no shortage of them; bunking off, as we called it then, now more commonly known as truanting, smoking, and at least two public real set-to fights with other boys for reasons I can't even remember.

Mr. J.P. Reynolds M.A., who had issues, as they say now, which would probably call for therapy of some kind, went at it with such enthusiasm that I cried in the toilets for half an hour. When I dropped my trousers and examined my behind in the toilet mirror, he had actually managed to inflict a few ugly red marks on it, and I even contemplated the then ultimate boy crime, going crying about it to your mum and dad. No one ever knew apart from a couple of friends, who urged me to report it to someone, but we were all vague as to who to report it to, and we knew well enough that telling any individual teacher would put the teacher in a difficult position.

My third time was the day before I left the school, just a few weeks after I'd turned eighteen. My last year was spent as a prefect, a pillar of the establishment, I suppose, though my return to the straight and narrow didn't really have anything to do with the beating I'd received. I'd just grown up, or was at least further on in that direction, and as I sat there, one benefit of adulthood dawned on me very powerfully.

As a boy, I'd had no say in either process or outcome. Now, while I was still locked into the traditional process, each senior boy saying a personal goodbye to the Head, I did have control of the outcome. I could tell Reynolds to his face in so many well-chosen words that he was a sadist and a brute who was not fit to be in charge of children, or I could go with normality, make a little small talk, shake his hand, take his best wishes and reciprocate them for him and the school, and depart. I did the latter, because I felt that, whatever his attitudes and standards were, I intended to keep to mine, and I hadn't forgotten his kindness on my first waiting chair experience. Perhaps the man was a Jekyll and Hyde character, and looking back, I suspect he was, but I no longer needed to care, and I didn't.

In late January, I had some hospital tests, as you know; I suppose this probably set off the rumours. In early March, I went to hear the results, and there I was in a waiting chair again, physically a fully-grown man, but in some ways that nervous boy all over again, just as unsure about the results and just as dubious about the concept of justice. The outcome was more second waiting chair than

147

first, I'm afraid, and unlike a beating, the issue won't disappear with the red marks.

But once again, I have adult privileges. Once again, I can't control the outcome, but I can control the process. It would be monstrously presumptuous of me to tell Jane, Sarah and Peter before telling you; they are much beloved daughter-in-law and grandchildren to me; to you, they are wife, daughter and son. And to be honest, the talk as I've heard it is a year at most, and spending that time with endless weeping and wailing and gnashing of teeth around me is a daunting prospect.

I am tired and growing more so by the day; I want and need support and love. And if I am now on my way back to Elaine, as it seems is the case, I might finish up feeling less like a fish out of water than I have since losing her.

So, with more regrets than I can express in words, I have to plant you on your own waiting chair, Philip. We both know that the evils of old-fashioned boyhood are unlikely to trouble you now, and I know well enough that this particular waiting chair isn't your first, by any means. But for this infernal lockdown, I could have told you face to face, but as you rightly say, that choice is no longer available and burying our heads in the sand about it achieves nothing.

I know Jane, Sarah and Peter very well, but not as well as you do. If you don't want to tell them until the endgame, probably a hospice, I would think, so be it. If you think they can handle it in the meantime, so be that too. But don't let that bit about Elaine give you the wrong impression; I love you all very much and not least you, my son, who have been and remain a constant source of pride and joy to your parents.

Love to you always,
Dad

June 6th.

Dear Dad,

I happened to catch sight of David Cullen on his return leg; he's a bit difficult to miss these days, so I can get back to you as soon as possible after receiving your letter.

I also sat on that chair three times, twice in Mr. Enfield's regime and once in Mrs. Hartson's. True, by then they couldn't hit you physically, but they had other methods. The only one I summoned up enough courage to tell you about was the third one, when Mrs. Margaret Hartson wanted to see me; the kids all called her 'Madge.' This was in Year 11, and I'd pretty much sorted out such petty criminality as my adolescence had contained by then. She wanted to congratulate me, as captain of the school under-16 rugby team, on winning the local schools' championship. Yes, we were going to be presented with the trophy in assembly, but nevertheless, she liked the personal touch, and I appreciated it. She had what the kids – boys and girls by then, of course - called 'dagger eyes' when she was annoyed; when she wasn't, she had a smile that could light up the whole room. She made me feel ten feet tall.

And what about the other two, I can hear you thinking. I'll tell you that face to face when we talk again, Dad, because we will talk again, I promise. I know you're adamant that you don't want any of us to put ourselves at risk, and no more do we want to risk infecting you, but things are relaxing and opportunities will come soon. If they don't, well our letter-writing skills are developing to the point where we can say what we want, can't we?

Yes, telling my family is my baby in the first instance, though I know well enough that Jane would be hurt and disappointed if I didn't involve her in passing on the news to the 'children,' who are, of course, children no more. So I'll share things out from the start by telling Jane. We can then decide between us when and what to tell Sarah and Peter.

My worst waiting chair yet, Dad, is the coming prospect of getting through life without you or Mum. That team captaincy which so wowed Mrs. Hartson was your work every bit as much as mine; your training, both in rugby and in dealing with other people, was what put me there. And there's been so, so much else. Every waiting chair I've ever faced, whatever the outcomes were, you've been there for me, sometimes more so than I really deserved.

I remember someone I knew once wondering how many English fathers have died without their sons ever telling them that they loved them. Millions, I suppose, on the old English ticket of men concluding that articulating such things is too emotional, too sentimental. Well, they can make their own decisions, but you're not going to be one of the never told, Dad. I love you dearly, I always have, and if you have to go, I'll move heaven and earth to make what has to happen as decent and painless as is humanly possible.

And when I can say that to your face, I will, and very soon.

Love, Philip

THE EDGE OF TRUST

I see young Ben Lockwood approaching the tall bushes on the far side of the running track at Harewood Sports' Centre. Some top athletes train in this place, and most prefer to do so with a degree of privacy. Ben passes the half way point of his 5000 metres training run, and I stop my watch. I've worked with this runner for nearly three years now, but even I find myself double taking at the time he's recording. Given a faster time on the second half, which he always does, he could record one of the best 5000 metres times in the U.K. this year. He could be heading for the U.K. team, which is why I'm allowed to bring him here from his Young Offenders' Institution.

He's passing the bushes. He could jump the fence behind them within seconds. He knows it and I know it, though neither of us has yet specifically mentioned it.

The YOI Governor, Ed Lakin, has mentioned it. When I took my case to him to take Ben to the best sports centre in the area for proper training, he listened, as he always does, even if he might then dismiss the request in crisp and pointed terms. His mouth straight lined, and his piercing dark eyes lasered across the desk.

'You're pushing your luck, Sam, you really are. Taking you off rosters occasionally for training the boy is one thing; putting that kind of temptation his way is another.'

'He may shortly be out anyway, Governor –'

The eyes flashed ominously.

'I don't know why you say that. I haven't heard anything.'

151

The hell Sam's mother Josie and her media friends were kicking up outside had been noticed, which Ed knows as well as I do, but you don't bandy words with Governor Lakin.

'He will almost certainly become a professional athlete, Ed, and that means professional facilities and some kind of new start for him. Isn't that what we're about?'

The eyes flashed again, the mouth tightened even more, and he flicked his papers about, a sure sign of thinking it over.

'O.K., Sam, but on your head be it, and I mean that. You're doing what I want officers to do, understanding inmates and making informed judgements, but informed means properly informed, or both you and us will be in the you-know-what.'

So far, so good, but the Governor has his limits, and the news I'm going to have to hand on to Ben when he finishes his training run is that he's got no chance of winning international representation this year. There are regional trials coming up, but Ben isn't going. YOI boys are not often selected for international running duty – in fact, I can't think of a single case in my twenty-two years' training - and the Governor is jittery about the likely press howls of outrage if Ben is selected. Ben is about to be disappointed; I already am. Coaches from YOI's rarely train potential champions; such places can be seen as career graveyards, fetching up with young hoodlums rather than promising schoolboys or university students.

I had a few bits of bother in my own youth, and this job was one of the few where that's actually an asset. I'm over twice their ages, literally old enough to be their father. But they don't try their stunts with me, because they know I know them all.

Ben Lockwood has been in here for nearly three years; he'll be 20 in a couple of months, and the only stunt he's ever tried on me is to dedicate himself to his athletics. He's developed a practised, professional running style, an easy, economical movement, a swaying but controlled rhythm. As he arrives in front of me, he's not even out of breath.

I tell him his time, and his blue eyes, which still speak of innocence even this far into his stretch, light up like headlamps and a big smile breaks across his face. Until he sees mine.

'I'm not going, am I?'

'No. I did my best, Ben. But they won't have it, not this time around anyway. All the same, that's an incredible time. Only two British men have done better this year so far, and they're both running for their country. You're making real progress, Ben.'

A sudden troubled, haunted look, one all too common for this boy.

'Only they won't let me show it, will they, Mr. Thorpe? Be a good boy and you'll get the chances. Doesn't work, does it?'

He's off to the changing room, and I'm cursing under my breath. What now? A question this job is asking me for the umpteenth time.

Ben Lockwood is polite, self-disciplined and hard-working, a potential athletic champion and a well-spoken, intelligent lad. So what's he doing in a YOI?

Ben was eight when his father Steve, aged 34, died when his motorbike hit an articulated truck on the M5. Ben's mother Josie bashed on as a single mother until Ben was 12 and she herself was 34, when she met a well-camouflaged vicious bastard called Malc Dalton. A year later, they married, and by the time Ben was 14, Dalton had started knocking both him and his mother about. It

153

was also about this time that Ben's interest in running started; since he knew it would take a while before he could match Dalton in physique, he thought he could at least try to better him in fitness which, given Dalton's lifestyle, wouldn't be too difficult.

For a while, they tried to live with Dalton's violence, because they knew that even if the police got as far as arresting Dalton, he was capable of charming his way out of it and then piling it on even thicker. However, the abuse worsened to sexual as well as physical, on both of them. Eventually, when Ben was 15, Josie planned their escape carefully, arranging for a friend to rent a flat for them and leaving for it in the middle of the night. Her friend put Josie in touch with a supportive organisation, and with their help, Josie contacted a lawyer to start divorce proceedings.

All was going well until some legal idiot sent Dalton a document with Josie's new address on it. Two months after Ben's sixteenth birthday, Dalton broke into the flat. He had started to set about Josie when Ben came out from the kitchen behind him and fetched him a huge blow on the back of his head with a large frying pan. As he staggered about, Ben hit him with the pan again; he dropped, catching the side of his head on the protruding arm of a metal chair. By the time the paramedics arrived, he was dead.

What Ben had done was not in dispute, but then the tug of war started, with one side arguing self-defence after years of abuse and the other, including Dalton's family and pub mates, talking about Josie's desertion and her failure to bring her son up properly. Eventually, Ben, now seventeen, went down for six years, the first three in a YOI.

The Dalton crew then over-reached themselves. Too lenient, they all screamed; they should lock the boy up for life meaning life. They should put him straight into an adult prison, where good-looking boys are really taught a lesson. Everyone knew what they meant.

But, of course, men like Dalton make enemies as well as intimidated friends, and it didn't take long for what Dalton really was to emerge; a whole catalogue of violence, reported and otherwise, in pubs, clubs and football grounds. And Josie found she was no longer ploughing a lonely furrow; several organisations and media people were weighing in with her, and she got the opportunity of widespread publicity concerning how she and Ben had been treated.

Now, near to Ben's transfer from the YOI to an adult prison, there aren't many left in the Dalton camp, and the chances are that he will not even transfer.

But, of course, the legal establishment doesn't like to admit its mistakes too easily. The hubbub to get Ben out is now deafening, but the Dalton lot are still doing their best, the latest argument being that Ben's running ability is giving him special status, an argument as essentially untenable as its predecessors, but one to which Governor Lakin feels susceptible. It could mean Ben at least transferring, and the prison regime could be disastrous for him very quickly.

Life seems to have something against this young guy, and arriving in the changing room as he emerges from the shower, his vulnerability and youth are all the more striking.

'Listen, Ben,' I say, sitting on a bench near him. 'You might not even be inside next year. Stick with it, right?'

The eyes meet me immediately, and the anger is all too clear.

'I appreciate what you've done for me, sir. It's just that it's not easy when you keep coming up against this

155

brick wall. We both know where I'm likely to be going, and how much running will I be able to do there?'

'I can't answer that, Ben. But don't give up hope, lad; not now, now you've come so far.'

He says very little on our way back to the YOI. He has told me sometimes about his conversations with his mother, and I know that Josie is deliberately down playing the possibilities of him getting out in the near future. I know why, too. He's been close to it several times now, and she wants to spare him going through it all again.

'One of these times, Sam,' she said to me once, 'will be one too many, and he'll do something stupid. He's a good lad, but he's still a lad.'

What I know and Josie doesn't is that he may be closer to getting out than he ever has been. The Governor has visitors arriving during the coming week, and I know there are nameless and faceless powers who are not at all keen on the publicity crackling around Ben Lockwood, a furore being fed by some expert journalists and publicists. They're even less keen on the potential material emerging from his transfer to an adult prison, and they quite like the idea of the system turning a young killer from knife murderer to international athlete. 'Look at the rehabilitation which YOI's can achieve!' will be the triumphant line. In my view, Ben was never really a criminal in the first place; he was a young boy doing the only thing he could do at the time to prevent his mother being beaten up or worse.

But none of that takes away from me the decision I have to make. Do I or do I not continue to take him to the sports centre? Do I trust Ben and his mother enough? Do I know enough about their friends outside?

Today is Thursday, the Governor's meeting is on Monday, and Ben's next full training session is next

Tuesday. If I forbid him his full run, how likely is he to ever trust me again? If he does scoot over the fence to a car or something arranged by Josie or her press pals, then even if I keep my job, the mutterings in the Staff Club will go on for ever afterwards, and no YOI boy will ever use the Centre again. And running with him is no answer; I can't live with his pace and he'd be over the fence before I could do anything about it.

By the time Tuesday arrives, I'm shorter on sleep than I was a week ago. It cannot be other than a battle when your entire professional integrity is at stake. But ultimately, I have to trust my instinct, born of long experience, and my instinct tells me Ben is trustworthy enough, and so is his mother, however fervent in his cause.

So when Ben is getting changed on Tuesday afternoon, it's in the Centre. I still don't know the outcome of the Governor's meeting yesterday; Ben doesn't even know there was a meeting. He's quiet, but then he usually is; unsurprisingly, he's not an ebullient kid.

We head out onto the fields; he jumps up and down to get his circulation going.

'You O.K.?' I say, and he nods, though there is a sudden glance away at something in the distance, which is unsettling.

We talk briefly about stride and rhythm, and then he's off, as controlled as ever, into his stride pattern as soon as he starts moving. Then, suddenly, about 400 hundred yards away, a quick glance backwards, as if to check I'm still there. I'm experiencing a moment of panic when my phone goes.

And it's the man himself, Governor Lakin, his voice for once almost friendly.

157

'Sam? I gather you're with Ben Lockwood now, aren't you?'

'Yes, Governor, I am. Why?'

'He's going out, Sam. And he's going out this Friday; they don't want to give the media weeks talking about it.'

'Bail? Parole?'

'Nope.'He sounds as if he might break into song, and that doesn't happen too often either. 'End of, Sam. They'd done all the paperwork when they got here. Remissions for good behaviour, mitigations for self-defence, they had it all worked out. Josie and her mob have really put the wind up them, let me tell you.'

'Have you told her?'

'Yes, I have.' he pauses; almost a sigh of delight. 'One of those rare moments, Sam. I've told her to keep schtum until he's out, when she'd be best advised to take him on a long holiday. She's coming to get him on Friday, and arranging things in the meantime. She might have press men camped on her lawn, but she and Ben won't be there.'

'So you want me to send Ben to you when he's finished?'

'No, Sam. You tell him. I'll see him afterwards; there's paperwork and stuff, when is there not? But you tell him.'

I can't help a quick gasp, and he knows what I'm gasping about.

'Yes, I know. It's not strictly procedure. But you're the guy who's kept the boy onside, Sam – even worked wonders with him. You've done the work, Sam. You tell him. And you both deserve it.'

I'm grinning as I click the phone off, and look towards Ben, thinking to wave him back. It takes me a few seconds to realise that he's not there.

My face feels as if the blood is draining out of it. He's jumped, he must have done. It can't be Josie; the Governor's just been talking to her. He's done a deal with someone with connections, and that's dangerous; connections don't come cheap.

And so, here I am running towards the trees, running in a panic like one more duped fool locking the stable door after the horse has bolted. Maybe I might just be in time to see the vehicle speeding off with its occupants having a good giggle at the demise of my professional reputation.

But then, professional I must still be, and security have to be told. I'm turning to my phone when I hear a weird noise, somewhere between a sob and a gasp, from a clump of bushes on my left. I move to the voice, and I don't suppose I've ever been as happy to see anyone in my entire life as I am to see Ben Lockwood.

Even if he is in a bit of a bad way, sprawled along the ground, with one hand clutching at his leg and a grimace of pain on his face.

'What happened, Ben?'

'Hamstring, sir. And I think it's a Grade 2 or even a Grade 3. I've had them before, but never as bad as this. It went so suddenly, I was dancing about with it, and then I fell on my knee, making it worse.'

A Grade 2 is a partial muscle tear; Grade 3 is complete. Either will put him out for weeks.

He will need a stretcher; I call for aid from inside the Centre. Maybe why doesn't matter at this moment, but it's that professional thing again.

'Hamstrings happen from overdoing it, Ben. You're on a balanced training programme. You shouldn't have hamstrings popping on you -'

'I've been doing extra gym stuff, sir. Maybe I have overdone it, but I need to get away from some of the

159

creeps. If you think I'm the blue-eyed boy inside...well, I'm not. It's only luck and a few friends who've stopped a beating.'

He's still clutching the back of his leg, a picture of misery. It seems the right moment.

'Well, as of this Friday, you won't be inside anyway. You're going out, Ben.'

The eyes raise immediately and scan my face. Am I having him on? Then he realises that I don't have people on about stuff like this, and his whole face lights up like a beacon.

'No bails, no paroles. Out. For ever. It's over, lad.'

As two guys and a stretcher approach over the field, one twenty-year-old is sitting on the ground sobbing his heart out. I put a hand on his shoulder.

'Get it all out of your system, lad; God knows, you're entitled. But the stretcher guys are here, and you'd better get on it, you can hardly stand up.'

He dries his eyes with his running top, and they've got him away in about two minutes flat. I follow him in, and concerned as I am for his injuries, there's something inside me which I know now will always be there. I've walked to the edge of trust and looked into the abyss, and there is still solid ground beneath my feet.

THE FELLOWSHIP OF VICTIMS

Berlin in the autumn of 1945 was a strange, desperate place. The remaining three million people in a city which once housed four and a half were mostly engaged in the most basic of human pursuits, a roof – any kind of roof – over the head and a subsistence of food.

Having been fighting across Europe since D-Day 1944, I felt drained and exhausted, at the ripe old age of twenty-two, but for the war against the Nazis, my vested interest remained. My mother was a Russian Jew who fled one of the many pogroms against the Jews in 1911, when she was ten years old. She had devoted herself to learning English even before leaving Russia, and she continued when the family were living five or six to a room in the East End. In 1919, she met and fell in love with a war-weary Englishman with only one hand, my father Leonard Railton, who had enough spirit and energy left in him to set up a small grocery business. Railton's Stores prospered; by the time I was born in late 1923 and named Leonard after him, he had three shops. They had waited until they could afford me and my education was very thoroughly attended to from the start. My mother realised the occupational potential of being bi-lingual, and her careful reinforcement of my conversations with her family ensured that I was fluent in Russian by my teens.

As a direct consequence, I was chosen as liaison officer with the adjacent Russians to my regiment's part of the British sector. However dodgy my colonel thought speaking Russian and coming from the East End were, I had the language and I think I'd proved by then that I wasn't too young to be incapable of diplomacy; most of the daredevil, glory boy types had got themselves killed by then anyway.

My sergeant was a quiet-spoken shrewd Lancastrian called John Spence, two years my senior, who'd been fighting alongside me ever since the perilous Normandy landings. We made our way to the improvised, ex-business premises office of the Russian regiment's liaison officer to talk about stray Brits or lost soldiers or any other issues the two armies needed to sort out. Of course, anything really important had to be reported back to our superiors, but these international meetings at least made us feel important.

And the Russian proved to be something of a surprise. I was expecting someone like my London relatives, who were, with a few spectacular exceptions, stubborn, sentimental, if tough as old nails, and tending to be awkward and monosyllabic with strangers.

But Alexander Lukashenko seemed, in nature, more English than Russian. He was a year older than me, lean, slightly-built and startlingly pale, as if permanently ill, though his manner contradicted this. In a bare office on Friedrichstrasse with a few tables, chairs and filing cabinets in it, big-windowed and dusty, probably once part of a department store, we discovered that he was as fluent in English as I was in Russian. I had carefully prepared a courteous Soviet style introduction, and he listened to it from behind his desk with mounting incredulity. When I'd finished, he replied in almost native English, an amused sparkle in the cool green eyes contrasting bizarrely with the alabaster complexion.

'Your Russian is excellent, Captain, and I return your greetings with all the cordiality with which they have been offered. Just don't call me bloody comrade, if you don't mind; I get enough of that as it is.'

162

His own sergeant, Koslov – no-one called him anything but Koslov – shot him one of those looks with which I was to become familiar. Koslov had no more than a smattering of English, but some instinct seemed to whisper in his ear when his boss said something he shouldn't. His manner towards Lukashenko was, in any case, jarring, as far as John Spence and I were concerned. John and I had been in tanks, dark forests and swamps together, shooting or being shot at, for what had felt like an eternity and we often didn't bother with 'sir' and 'sergeant' – it was Len and John. On the way back to the British sector, he spoke his mind.

'You know, it's almost as if that NCO of his is keeping tabs on him.'

'Yes, I thought that,' I said. Koslov's eyes were constantly on his Major; he sometimes even looked over Lukashenko's shoulder to see what paperwork he was doing. I felt a spark of curiosity and was oddly relieved – I had begun to think that my capacity for normal reactions had gone, after having seen more in a year than any man should have to see in a lifetime. And, for once, curiosity and duty coincided. 'We need to know as much as you can glean about who and what is going on over there,' the Colonel had said.

As it happened, an opportunity presented itself almost immediately. At our very next meeting on the Russian side, Lukashenko took a phone call.

'Koslov, Commissar Bulgarin needs a driver urgently and you're the only one available. Report to central base immediately and you can pick me up when you've finished there.'

Koslov had the impertinence to hesitate, but another curiosity about Lukashenko was his patrician, English ex-public schoolboy manner, an expectancy about being obeyed which I suspect Koslov found intimidating.

Lukashenko looked down his nose, quite literally, at his sergeant, refusing to speak again until Koslov had gone. Then he sat back in his chair, produced a packet of cigarettes and offered me one. I didn't hesitate – everyone smoked in those days, and good cigarettes were hard to find.

'Tedious Party bastard,' Lukashenko said, in English. 'He watches and reports on me, you know, Leonard. It is Leonard, isn't it?'

'Yes,' I said, taken aback; such familiarity was rare.

We broke several rules by exchanging our stories. His parents were distant cousins of the last Tsar himself, though not so distant that they couldn't afford a comfortable country mansion on the outskirts of Moscow, where Alex had been brought up. Since the 1917 Revolution, both his parents had died – not shot by the Bolsheviks, as so many of the Tsar's family had been, but simply, as Alex put it, 'harried to death,' with soldiers billeted in their home and much of their wealth 'requisitioned.' Alex himself had been forced into the Red Army.

'I've fought the Bosch as hard as any of them, right across Russia and Eastern Europe,' he said. 'And now they pretend to concede enough to let me do this, though in truth they don't have anyone else who could do it anyway. I was sent to school in England – 'English public school education is the best in the world,' my father pronounced. I miss the old man, acutely at times.' So he was an ex-English public schoolboy, though his patrician ways didn't stop him from listening to my own story.

When I'd finished, he sighed and said, 'I would love to be able to reassure you, Leonard, that life has improved for your mother's people under the new 'rule of the proletariat,' but I would be telling lies and my mother always told me I wasn't very good at that. I suppose that's why that bastard Koslov relays to the KGB everything I do. I can say the words they want me to say, but I can't make them convincing. Only my officer ability has saved me so far from Stalin's gulags, but now the fighting has stopped, my inability to fawn and talk nonsense will probably bring about my downfall.'

We already knew something of what Stalin was doing to his own people, and I felt a growing sympathy for this naturally good-mannered man who simply happened to be in the wrong country at the wrong time. Being a Jew to the English and an Englishman to the Jews, with distrust and suspicion emanating from both sides, I knew something of displacement. My father adamantly refused my mother's family's demands to bring me up in the Jewish faith; he and my mother called the bluff and married quietly in a registry office. It had been forgiven, but not forgotten. But, as the concentration camp horrors filtered through to us, I had never felt so acutely my Jewish connection. Alexander's experiences taught my gradually embittering mind that being victimised and discriminated against was not just the fate of the poor and under-represented, and identifying my East End self with an upper-class Russian with royal blood in his veins was not as ridiculous as it might seem. Maturity is about seeing the greys between the blacks and the whites.

It also dawned on me that Alexander's constant pallor was not because of illness; it was because, for all his urbane attitudes and bravery in the field, he lived with perpetual terror. And I thought that, if Stalin's camps resembled Hitler's camps, he had good reason to be terrified.

The next three weeks permitted little in the way of leisurely communications; items of business and complications were growing every day, and Koslov was never called away again. We had the impression the man had arranged it so; even a Commissar couldn't countermand the KGB.

Our last meeting was at the British liaison office in West Berlin, a slightly plusher affair than the Russian one, though not by much. Ours was a commandeered hotel, the furniture a little more elegant and the carpet a little less threadbare, but it was dusty, draughty and had the general run down look which had settled over all Berlin like a cloud of depression.

He leaned towards me.

'Do you play chess, Leonard?'

'Yes, sometimes; perhaps, with leisure and opportunity –'

'I have to play my Black Queen. I have no other choice.'

He leaned even closer, his breath tobacco and vodka. He was almost in tears, begging me to listen carefully and understand. He lowered his voice, even though Koslov was two rooms away, John Spence busily entertaining – and compromising - him with the malt whisky he would never see on the eastern side.

'The blackest but most powerful move, the risk of dragging a trusted friend into trouble to get me out of it. Believe me, Leonard, I do it only because I am checked almost to mate.'

I waited; he seemed to struggle with his breathing.

'You will not see me again. Tomorrow I am to report to KGB Berlin base with Koslov; he will denounce me, alleging fraternisation and other nonsense, and I will be flown out. I will be in a labour camp within the week. We are in an endgame, Leonard.'

I had to think quickly, but the times were like that; normal processes of looking at the ideology and the practicality had to be telescoped into minutes. Ideologically, on the face of it, I had no common cause to

166

make with Lukashenko; he was related, however distantly, to an oppressive royalist regime which had enslaved and terrorised its people for generations. But I thought of the Russian soldiers pounding into Jewish settlements to do what they did, and then Alex Lukashenko in his labour camp being slowly worked and starved to death, and I saw victims, just as John and I had been seeing all the way across Europe, victims in their countless thousands displaced, impoverished and murdered, just as my mother's family would have been had she not left Russia and come to England, and a feeling of fellowship with all the victimised rose in me again.

The practicality, in this case, was not too complicated. If he applied for political asylum, the Russians would be furious at a time when we needed their co-operation. If he simply disappeared, no-one would be particularly perturbed; people were, all over Europe, with terrifying regularity, and had been for some years.

Alex's talk of chess reminded me that, in that game as in life, a bold and simple bluff, confidently executed, could sometimes equal many more ponderous and elaborate strategies. I made up my mind.

I moved to the door and called for Koslov in Russian. He appeared, rosier in the cheeks than he had been; John was standing behind him grinning.

'Sergeant, the Major and I have to go down to our archives to check on some details of missing officers. I can get authorisation for him and him only. Please remain here for a few minutes; I'm sure Sergeant Spence will entertain you.'

Koslov looked suspicious, as he always did, but in this instance, there wasn't much he could do. As I turned away, John and I exchanged a look of total

167

understanding, meaning Koslov must be kept where he was at all costs for half an hour.

Downstairs, the labyrinthine basement currently housed all the British records pertaining to this part of Berlin, but leading off from it, and known only to a select group of officers, were doors and passages leading to underground chambers, initially used by the more affluent Germans to protect themselves from the Allied bombing; more recently used by Germans who didn't want to be captured and were seeking to make their way out of Berlin by the already established Nazi escape routes through the sewers and cellars.

Some of these subterranean chambers had only recently been vacated and were still reasonably well-appointed, with beds, chairs, tables and sometimes even desks. In one of these, Alex and I stopped and I looked into his now even paler face.

'We will tell them you have done a runner, Alex, meaning the Russian agents in West Berlin, scores of them, will be looking for you. We will get you civilian clothes and fly you out on one of the routine flights to London in a few days' time. In due course, you will be quietly granted asylum; there will be some interrogation, but nothing too exacting, I suspect. In the meantime, make yourself as comfortable as you can.'

He grabbed my hand; it was discomfiting to see the tears glistening in those normally urbane green eyes.

Upstairs, I spoke to Koslov again.

'I regret to say that your major has absconded into West Berlin, Sergeant, on the excuse of a toilet visit, leaving his uniform jacket behind him. I will notify the proper authorities at once, and I would think, even in the chaos of this city, we may well find him.'

Koslov looked from me to John and back again. John's hand was tightening on his holster gun; John was a muscular and now highly experienced professional soldier who had fought his way across Europe, and so was I. We regarded Koslov dispassionately. He accepted the situation, because there wasn't much else he could do.

'You will be hearing from us again, Englishmen, and at a very high level. You may not find yourself in post for very much longer.'

John snorted abruptly, and fingered the whisky glass Koslov had been using.

'I suspect you, too, may have your difficulties, comrade,' he said, in English, though Koslov understood perfectly. The Russians took a dim view of their officers drinking on duty, and also buying liquor from the allies; Koslov had regularly done both.

'I'm sure your chums in the KGB will understand, Koslov,' I said.

The man's face went an odd puce-like colour and stormed out; neither John nor I ever saw him again.

The security men forbade me from seeing or associating with Lukashenko from then on, for their own professional if unfathomable reasons. On the day his three man escort party came to take him to the plane, I went down to his little improvised quarters when I knew he was temporarily elsewhere in the basement and left him an English ten pound note, making clear this was a gift from me and not to be entered into any official record. I wanted him to have something of direct and immediate use to him when he arrived in England. Ten pounds was much more then that it is now, and I was being paid reasonably well by the standards of the time with little or no opportunities for spending.

The next day, I visited that cell for the last time. He had somehow contrived, God knows how, to leave a tiny vase with a bunch of flowers in it, a startling, rather incongruous splash of colour in the bleak little room, and a chess piece, the Black Queen. His note said, 'sometimes the darkest gamble produces the best result. Bless you, my good friend.'

I still have the Black Queen in a cabinet at home. Lukashenko anglicised his name – to what, I'll keep quiet about - and became, eventually, a Professor of History; we met occasionally until his death five years ago. He was far from the only person trying to get out of the Russian sector who John and I helped over the next few months, before the Army decided that we had done our bit and demobbed us. But Alex's escape, perhaps because he was so different in background from me, particularly expressed my feeling of fellowship for the victims of our times as well as the intrinsic value of it for all times.

I am now a widower, living in a comfortable 'retirement apartment' in Devon and, to my utter astonishment, celebrated my ninetieth birthday last year. There is very little left in my appearance or demeanour which would suggest the active young Army officer, except, perhaps, a certain stiffness in the back and neck. Most people in our residence are treated with respect; when, for whatever reason, they are not, I can still summon up enough eloquence and spirit to mount a defence. After a war, the fellowship of victims tends to stick with you.

The late Leonard Railton, completed August 2013.

THE UNPLAYABLE

I met him on Wednesday, August 15th 1996, by the frozen food counter in Sainsbury's. I saw him picking things up, peering at them, and putting them back. A woman in the next aisle was gazing at him with an odd mixture of maternity and lust.

The nineteen-year-old Lex Winter, Lex short for Alex, reserve team professional footballer, was as gorgeous a youth as I'd ever seen. Almost exactly six feet tall, naturally dark-skinned, with jet black short hair and disconcerting blue green eyes, he had a perfect torso fully emphasised by a thin light blue top, bare untattooed arms, and leg-hugging jogging bottoms. Never mind a punter, I thought; I'd do him for free.

Yes, at the time, I was rent. Ian Sims, twenty-one years old, failed student and failed genius of cuisine. Once the lack of academic brain had been established, it was sweating in some tyrant's kitchen for sod all or the game. The game, for the moment, won.

False modesty to hell, I was as cute as a basket of kittens, big brown hazel eyes, flashing white teeth, blondish hair I'd spend hours on, and a few other decidedly non-kittenish accoutrements as useful professional equipment. I'd lost contact with all the family except my aunt, Roz Forbes, drama lecturer and my dad's younger sister, who called herself the black cow of the family, bohemian, chain-smoking, foul mouthed. The last time I'd visited her in her city flat, a kind of Bedouin tent with a roof on, she looked at me and said, 'Ian, darling, I do believe you're on the fucking game.' I

171

wondered how she knew and begged for her silence. She looked me up and down.

'I don't shop people, sweetheart, even to my dear brother. Or should that be especially? But be careful, my lovely. Be bloody careful.'

Lex's eyes flicked at me and stayed just too long.

'Too much choice?' I said, and I got the eyes full on. I had to catch my breath.

'What are you supposed to do with this stuff?' he said, as if we were already mates.

We fumbled on for a few minutes, something about the landlady of his so-called 'digs' being away on holiday and him now 'pissed off with pizza and Chinese,' but it was all irrelevant flannel and we both knew it. We were in my place, a shag nest by the river, in thirty minutes and naked in forty. By then, I was pretty good at finding out soon enough what really floated a guy's boat, and often it had to be a matter of finding out. Some didn't have the words, some didn't have the nerve, and some didn't know, believe it or not. There had to be protection if needed – Aids was still very much in consciousness in 1990.

Otherwise, whatever. The graphic details of this session with Lex would take too long to go into; it seemed, for him, like a dam bursting, both mentally and physically. The main surprise about it, from my point of view, was that he was mainly submissive; I say mainly for the sake of accuracy, because there are few entirely one way or the other, whatever the stereotypes, and believe me, I should know. How much that squares with the image of macho footballers, I don't know, but I could see the conflict in him between what turned him on and what he thought should. I worked carefully on him with the benefits of long experience, and his beautiful, athletic body reacted to me like a man in a desert taking a drink.

172

After some expenditure of time and energy, we lay together for a few minutes. He knew normal gay etiquette made it my turn and I had to remind myself that this one was pleasure, not duty; not every punter worries too much about my turn. He surprised me with his expertise and obvious enjoyment of teasing me, carefully, expertly, back and front; he teased and teased, taking me to the edge and back again, until I was gasping and begging to be allowed to come, and when I did, I closed my eyes and went wherever that place is longer and higher than I could remember having done for weeks.

So we lay together again, this time with that strange post coital thing of two naked men realising they actually know next to nothing about each other.

'What do you do?' I said, for the sake of saying something.

'I'm a pro footballer.'

'Oh, right.' I nodded slowly. I'd had everything, up to and including astronauts. Why they feel they need to impress their whore, I never could understand. But they do.

'No, I am. Reserve team at the moment. Contract until twenty-one. Good money, but harder work than most people think.'

'I suppose.'

Then I made a mistake. He'd just mentioned working for a living, reminding me that I did too, so I flicked on my answer phone to get the messages.

'Hi – saw your ad and picture. Like it. I'm on town on Wednesday p.m.; how about something? I usually top; maybe a little CP with afters? Nothing heavy. Talk to you soon.'

'Hello. I don't know how happy you are topping middle-aged guys – real sub stuff, for me. Make me obey; anything, I mean anything –'

An odd choking shout sounded on my right; Lex was standing up, looking down on me, his eyes blazing. I flicked the machine off.

'Rent. God, you're fucking rent. This is a set-up, right? Pay up or the papers? Bastard – I thought you were just a guy –'

By this time, I'd got to my feet too and was trying to put my arms round him.

'No, fuck off,' he said, unconvincingly, pushing distractedly against me. 'How much do you want? I've got cash –'

'Lex, no –'

The split personality, aggression and submission, wildness and gentleness, which soon became familiar, then showed itself in all its spectacular opposition. He squared up, and suddenly I could see the muscles in the shoulders and arms, the total absence of spare flesh, more vividly than ever. He punched me on the cheek, only just missing my eye, and I saw red myself. No punter, I'd decided long ago, was ever going to knock me about. I punched him back, hitting almost exactly the same spot. For a minute or two, we massaged our wounds, both of us, I think, surprised at the force and pain of the blows. Then we looked at each other and dissolved into giggles like two little kids. We weren't much more, when all's said and done. I grabbed the moment.

'I didn't do you as a punter, Lex. I did you because I fancied you like hell. And I was right.'

From then on, it seemed that we were made. I'd become a cynical bastard, as indifferent to punters as most of them were to me, but he'd pressed a button which I hadn't realised was still there. I even got onto boring old football, just to sound interested.

'I want to get to be something like... ,' he said, mentioning the name of a famous footballer, I assumed, though it meant nothing to me.

'The boss says that guy is unplayable.' Now there was real enthusiasm in his voice; the whole spasm of temper had faded, like a kid after a tantrum.

'Unplayable?'

'You know. Impossible to stop. He scores goals for fun. That's what I want to be. Unplayable.'

We continued to see each other off and on, precariously, Lex terrified that the media would somehow detect his regular visits; reserve team player or not, the death of Justin Fashanu in 1988 meant the subject of gay footballers was still high on the media agenda and Lex was paranoid about being followed or 'shopped.' It didn't seem to occur to him that the most obvious person to shop him would be me, and his instinctive, if mysterious, trust in me restored something of my severely battered self-belief. He didn't like the way I earned a living - understandably enough, I suppose. When I asked him what he would suggest, we would have one of his long, distracted sulks, like a kid whose ball has been pinched.

'If I make the big time, the hundred grand a week stuff, that'll be that, Ian.'

Two or three months in, he started getting games in the full team rather than the reserves, and bringing me press cuttings about his matches; seeing me, he said, had improved his game. At first, the logic of this mystified me. But I think, with me, the guilt and recrimination had gone; he could allow his submissive side to be satisfied. Guys whose lives often need them to be aggressive and assertive, which is most of them, can lose off the gentler side, the desire to give themselves to and be enjoyed by someone; it becomes associated with guilt and fear, especially the fear of vulnerability, in a world where many

175

people are more likely to find male vulnerability exploitable and contemptible than engaging. Lex came to me, had his fill, and went back out to play the game he needed to play, in more ways than one.

I began to ache for him when he wasn't there, and to resent the guys I had to deal with. Lex was incredibly athletic, fastidiously clean and fantastic looking; everyone else paled beside him. He told me sometimes about needing to tell stories to keep the guys happy.

'You should hear the way they talk about women,' he would say. 'In the dressing room, talking about their lays as if they've waving their cocks at each other. 'I gave it one straight off. Hungry, man.' 'It was a woof-woof, right enough, but it blew a beautiful job.' It. I fucked it. The Thing. But if any guy dares to talk about making them the 'its,' they're, like, 'oh, gross, man, gay is so gross.'

Then everything changed very rapidly, as it sometimes does. He arrived in a state of real excitement, his face lit up. He was going to be transferred, he said, into another club in the same league, except the manager had more or less guaranteed him first team football. And a lot more money.

'Come with me, Ian. You and me. Get out of this. I need you with me; I can't do it without you. Come with me.'

I hesitated, and he was hurt. He thought I wasn't convinced about the money and showed me the contract. Eye-stretching as the pay was, I still needed time to think, provoking another protracted sulk, which we got out of with a bathroom session – bathrooms had enormous potential, and Lex liked variety.

While he lay in my arms afterwards, I told him how difficult it had been to make myself free and independent, how he was the only person in the world I would even

176

think about giving that up for, but I had to have a little time and space.

I needed, for once, to talk to someone older, so I phoned Roz. She listened without interrupting, as she always has.

'I'm 95% sure I should go for it, Roz. What do you think?'

A kind of snort sounded down the line.

'Heavens, sweetheart, I'm no reed to lean on. My relationship history is like a battlefield after the battle, and all the corpses are me. Your dad could tell you if you asked him; in fact, he'd probably tell you even if you didn't ask him.'

'He might if he was talking to me.'

A heavy silence. 'Oh, Ian, darling.'

A vivid image came to my mind of my father staring up at me from his favourite armchair, his thin face pale and his eyes narrowed in the certainty of his utter contempt. Even now, those last few days could force tears. I tried to speak, but Roz got there first.

'Listen, Ian, you've always been a strong, determined little bugger, and if this guy isn't for you, someone will be. Get off the game, darling, because that will only ever last for a while before it starts to destroy you. How do I know, never mind how I know. Give Lex a go, sweetheart. Sometimes the chance is worth taking. I've had a few fuck up on me, yes, but while they lasted, I was having a ball.'

Roz clinched it. Lex and I put down a deposit on a flat about thirty miles from his club. He told them he was in a flat share and that's all he wanted for the moment. He was twenty years old; no-one thought much about it. We found a greater bliss and peace in that place than either of us had thought possible. It was a good deal bigger than my little shag nest, and I appointed myself in charge of décor and equipping the place. In the very centre of town, where people drifted in and out in their thousands and no-one noticed who came and who went, we lived our dream, and even the downside – Lex was an untidy sod, unused to regular meal times and not good at planning the next day, and I dare say I had my own set ways after being essentially alone for so long – was fascinating, revelatory, liberating.

By late 1992, we were a couple in every sense of the term that mattered, though even then, problems remained. Other members of the team had women who came to watch them and went to club dos with them, and Lex's youth and inexperience were wearing thin to explain his lack of a partner. He kept on with the line that he hit the town well away from the club so as not to get into the papers.

We had to have some kind of social life, and for that we relied almost entirely on my friends, some of whom remained on the game. Sex workers develop a kind of ethic of their own when it comes to the punters; even if you think you might get paid for going to the media with a 'name,' you know well enough that your business will be ruined for ever afterwards, because no one will trust you any more. Names are also likely to have squads of lawyers behind them. Discretion is practical politics as well as professional etiquette, and I wasn't too concerned about them shopping Lex. In any case, none of them could prove anything.

In mid-November 1999, we met up with Rick Pierce and his new lover Mark Southern. Rick had that elastic, high jumper's build which some guys are crazy about. He'd dipped in and out of prostitution after running from an oppressive Northern household; for a good while, he pretended the 'I only do it for money and I'm not really gay' line. Those guys do exist, yes, but he wasn't really one of them; a punter we had in common once described him to me as a 'really thirsty boy; I swear he'd do it just for the hell of it.' Mark worked in a hotel restaurant, the same hotel which Rick occasionally used for picking up. Mark was quiet and dark; he smiled incessantly, if enigmatically. Their flat was very similar to ours, with a balcony and a view; we all felt at home. Both being 'foodies,' Mark and I got on well enough, though something about him disturbed me, perhaps the way those little dark eyes darted about and wouldn't meet mine. He and Rick had first got it together in the hotel gents, risking Mark getting the sack; Rick described him to me as a 'sweet, uncomplicated guy who walks the wild side now and then; enough said.'

Late at night, after a drink or two, Rick looked at Lex and smiled.

'Now, tell me to butt out, Lex, but I only ever look at the sports back pages when a sexy picture catches my eye. The other day, that's what happened, and the guy with the oiled thighs on show didn't just look like you, he had the same name. How's that happen, Lex?'

We looked at each other, reaching a mutual decision; sooner or later, we thought, this had to happen, and it might as well be now, with guys who were friends enough to trust. Lex had had a drink, and I thought his pleasure at relaxing his secret was mostly about that, until, only a week later, he phoned me in mid-afternoon.

'Ian, I'm coming home with Brent Morrison.'

'Oh, God. What – to eat?'

Brent Morrison was a name I knew well enough by then, the captain of Lex's team, a guy in his mid-thirties playing out a solid career before heading into management. I knew he was married, with three young kids. He'd been magic with Lex from the first, advising him, encouraging him, showing him around. Lex knew he

179

helped the young players as part of his job; he balanced the taciturn Welsh manager in the familiar hard man, soft man combination, but he appreciated Brent all the same.

'He asked if he could visit where I lived; I couldn't think how to put him off. Maybe, after Rick and Mark, we could start – you know – taking it on?'

So Brent came to dinner, and said nice things about our place and my food. Lex and I looked at each other in the kitchen, question marks on both our faces, wondering whether the guy had worked it out. He was a big man, calm-eyed and curiously graceful on his feet, relaxed with himself and others.

A big, verbal coming out proved to be unnecessary. Lex and I were very easy with each other by then; we touched a lot, kissed each other casually, exchanged looks to check on how the other felt. In our own place, it would have taken a guy a lot less sensitive to people than Brent Morrison not to work out what we were all about.

The crucial moment happened quite incidentally. I put Lex's coffee down in front of him; he was finicky about his coffee, having it just the way he liked it. He sipped it and smiled, putting his hand on the back of my neck and pulling my face down to kiss. We had, just for a second, forgotten Brent was there. We both realised simultaneously, and his eyebrows went up as two anxious faces turned suddenly in his direction.

'Don't worry,' he said. 'It's under my hat for now. It comes out – you come out – when you judge the moment and the ground's been prepared a bit. I knew Justin Fashanu; I liked him. That's not going to happen to anyone in my team.'

Lex and I were both blown away with the idea that at last, we had a friend inside football. I even listened to them both explaining more about the game, to have a better idea of what Lex actually did day by day.

So the hammer in my guts was all the greater when, less than a week later, in my nearest store, Lex's name was plastered all over the local paper.

'Town's Young Pro Living With Rent Boy,' it said, in big black letters. Seven words, and I had to read them again and again, eyes flickering across the page to try and make myself believe it was really happening. 'A family friend – ' family friend? Who the hell? – 'describes the relationship as having lasted for some time. 'Lex Winter has always been gay, as far as I know,' he said. 'He hasn't come out because football won't let him come out'.' Well, right enough for that, I thought. But the identity of the family friend tormented me; I wondered wildly if it could be Roz Forbes.

I dashed back to the flat and Lex was already there, sitting on the sofa, pale and bewildered. It was only just after ten in the morning. He'd seen the paper in the garage when he got his petrol and turned right back, thinking that the ground would already be swarming with reporters – as it was.

'I can't believe it,' he said, in the half-strangled voice that normally precedes the long sulk. 'Brent Morrison. I trusted the bastard, I really did. The skip. Of all people.'

I was just about to agree with him, with an enormous sense of relief that my aunt was off the hook, when I made myself reflect that, if I could jump to such rapid and devastating conclusions, perhaps he could too.

'We don't know, Lex. 'Family friend' is hardly him, is it?'

The first knock on the door coincided almost exactly with the first ring of the phone, both of them immediately crushing any notions we might have that the media would still be working out exactly where we lived. Someone had told them that as well.

181

'Lex?' someone shouted from behind the door, and the use of his first name by a disembodied, unknown voice had a sinister edge to it. 'If Lex Winter is in there, we're offering the chance for you to put your side of the story. Don't let them have it all their way, Lex. Come out and talk to us.'

'Stay quiet,' I whispered to him. 'Stay very quiet.'

For a minute or so, he did, then he lost his head, for some reason, and stamped out on to the balcony to see if anyone of them were outside. The shouts, along with the whirl and clatter of cameras, started as soon as he stepped out. I saw his frame silhouetted against the increasing brightness of the morning, his back held awkwardly, frozen as if arrested by a beam of light.

I dragged him back in; we retreated to the bedroom, making sure every door was locked which could be. For over an hour, we lay beside each other on the bed, frozen, ignoring the knocks, shouts and phone buzzes. Then a different tone sounded, and I saw it was my mobile. I let it take a message, and picked it up afterwards. It was Rick, speaking as if someone had shut him in a cell.

'Ian, it was Mark. He's devastated. Late night at the club, blabbering to some guy he'd just met who turned out to be from the Sentinel. He's quiet as a mouse a lot of the time, but when he takes what he takes and puts booze on top of it – Ian, mate, I'm so sorry. Come to us. At least pick up on me, Ian, for fuck's sake....'

At that moment, I couldn't have talked to him – I couldn't have talked to anyone. I remember it registering that the press men can't have had the number of my mobile, because Rick's was the only call I'd had in the last two hours. How long it would have been before we'd taken action of some kind, I don't know, but we noticed the noise outside the flat door dying down rapidly, and then a different kind of knock sounded, more muted, less in your face.

'Lex and Ian? It's Brent, Brent Morrison. I think I can help.'

We let him in and locked the door behind him.

'O.K.,' he said, settling himself into an armchair. Apart from a slightly faster pace of talking, he didn't seem disturbed at all.

'The manager of the apartment block is out there with a couple of policemen. Residents have been screaming blue murder. They will at least make that lot retreat out of the building, so we've got a little breathing space.'

He appeared to be considering something for a moment; he was the kind of man who always tended to think before he spoke.

'Firstly, I'll tell you what the club wants you to do. The club wants me to take Lex back with me – just Lex - for a press conference early this afternoon, where we're going to say Ian's your flat mate, you've only known him for a few weeks, you didn't know what he was up to, their source was a young gay on the make – we'll imply blackmail – and then the club's lawyers will look at legal action if the papers persist.'

He looked up and saw the expressions on our faces. We were both momentarily struck dumb.

'Now,' and he looked straight into our faces, 'I'll tell you what I think you should do. You both have cars parked in that underground car park that serves the building?'

We nodded.

'They might know what Lex drives, but they certainly won't know what you drive, Ian. Go down in the lift while you have the chance, leave in Ian's car with Lex head

183

down on the back seat, go to some relative or friend they can't possibly know – can you think of anyone?'

Lex still looked bewildered, shell-shocked almost, but I leaned forward and nodded vigorously; yes, I certainly could think of someone.

'Then take a few days to think it through. It should be what you want to do, not what people can bounce you into. You need time. We'll tell them you've gone to ground and we don't know where.'

We agreed so completely and readily with Brent's idea – we were both very young and very frightened – that we didn't stop to worry about whether the club would take it out on Brent, though he left soon after that to take up a managerial post, and I think he'd probably already fixed that up. Big thick footballers is just one more sporting cliché.

We fled to Roz's for a few days, and she, bless her, was delighted to have us.

'Thank God, if She really is up there. I was going out of my mind. I didn't dare phone in case they were tracking – they do that, you know? Now we'll take it easy and think it over, boys.'

Two days later, Brent Morrison phoned me on my mobile, a number which he'd clearly kept strictly to himself, and he gave us the club line, hastily agreed by manager, chairman and backers. The club would buy out Lex's contract in full, all four years of it, to prevent anything going to court; they were afraid we might sue for unfair dismissal, Brent said. The condition was that Lex and I needed to simply disappear out of their lives for ever.

That night, we mulled it over around Roz's huge antique mahogany dining table, after Roz and I had joined forces to produce a very special meal – 'whatever has to be decided, we can at least do it on a pleasantly full stomach,' she said. Lex talked hesitantly, softly, the way he does when something is really on his mind. Roz and I watched and listened, but she had hold of my hand under the table and she squeezed it from time to time.

'If we sell the flat as well, we'll be fine to set up somewhere else. Maybe Ian could start a restaurant, where he can be the boss, like he's always wanted. I just can't face it, guys; the abuse, the spitting, the faces, every time I take a corner, every time I go near the touchline.

The dressing room mocking; the turned backs. There are gay pros; I know by their eyes, every changing room I've ever been in has at least one set of those eyes. Mine meet theirs; I know, he knows, and neither of us do anything about it. Yes, they'll be some on our side, but how many of them are going to be there, in the ground, when I have to go out and play?'

So the restaurant it was, and still is, twenty years on. I went into my business as the boss, which is the best way to do it. Lex had a ten-year, highly successful career as a model. When I first suggested the idea, he practically laughed himself into a fit, then I told him about the friends I had who'd said how incredible he'd be at it. He still resisted; he was adamant he wouldn't do nude stuff or porn, and I said he wouldn't have to. Lex by then, in his early twenties, with his dark looks and perfectly toned and proportioned body, was a clothes horse for the stuff many companies wanted to sell, and when he got more confidence with it, he did a few topless sessions for the gay papers. But the picture which almost every gay man – and quite a few women – had on their walls for a good while was the one he did for a certain underwear company. Iconic is a much over-used word, but iconic is what it was.

Lex in his early forties is a little bit beefier, but he can still kick a ball about and does charity matches

185

occasionally. My father is no longer with us, but my mother and I have picked up the pieces and I see her from time to time.

Twenty-eight years after we met, civil partnerships and same sex marriage have been made legal and discrimination against gay people has been made illegal. In almost every walk of life, including some very famous names indeed, gay people have felt able to come out to be and live as they are.

But since the suicide of persecuted Justin Fashanu in 1988, not a single solitary example yet exists of an out gay top rank professional footballer. For the gay world, football, the most widely supported sport in the world, remains the unplayable, still locked in its own bigoted and anachronistic isolation.

MINDING YOUR OWN

Steve Mullen generally regarded his job as a doddle, a falling on the feet; not quite a sinecure, but not far off. He watched a screen all day. Easy, but not very interesting. The pictures were almost always the same - the building's front entrance, the alley going down the side to the car park at the back, and overlooking the car park. The fancy title it came with was Security Manager. He would laugh about it with Harry Field, at change over; they handled day and night shifts between them, two weeks at a time.

'Steve,' Harry would say, 'we both get to be boss. Two chiefs and no bloody Indians.'

The block was all offices. Five storeys, with three or four offices on each one; lawyers, insurance, local paper, that kind of thing. Nobody kept anything but petty cash on the premises, nobody ever slept over. Steve sometimes wondered what they were afraid of, someone breaking in and walking off with the paper clips, maybe. But then, the operation wasn't exactly high-tech security either.

After two years, Steve had only twice had to contact the police, once when a bunch of lads were pissing about – literally – in the car park and once when a rough sleeper got in through the side door and looked like he was sniffing something up. There were a few explanations to be made on that one, the trouble being that the side door was supposed to be a fire escape, emergency only, but people leaving used it to cut down the alley to the car park, leaving it open behind them.

Then the caretaker failed to notice and lock it before he went.

Steve thought of it as the kind of job which would have suited his old man.

'Best rule in life, son, is mind your own business and don't get involved in anyone else's,' he'd say, fag and pint to hand. 'Don't get tangled up in other people's problems. Watching on, that's the best way.'

The old man practised what he preached, too, even before he became an old man. He watched live football, but never played it. As did Steve. He played a bit in his teens but soon it was too much effort, getting kicked, all that mud and water. But Joe Mullen went beyond football; he detached himself from everything. They were walking home from the pub once when Steve was sixteen, and they saw Tom Foster, a middle-aged pub 'regular,' getting mugged by two young men not much older than Steve. Joe and Tom were on at least nodding terms; they'd had a drink and a chat sometimes.

Steve thought he and Joe could at least have disturbed those lads enough to drive them off, but Joe kept right over on his side of the street, pretending not to see. As soon as he was out of sight, he phoned the police, fair enough, and it didn't turn out too serious, they just took Tom's cash, and landed him a couple in the guts.

But it sewed doubts in Steve's mind. When they got home, he said 'We should have helped there, Dad, don't you reckon?'

Joe was in his chair with a fag on; he gave Steve a sideways look.

'I've got a dodgy back and you're a long skinny squit of a kid. We phoned; that's enough. Believe me, son, keeping out of it's the best way.'

Tom didn't see it like that; he stopped speaking to Joe and no-one else seemed much impressed either. Not long after, Joe stopped going to the pub altogether. It drove Meg Mullen crazy, having him sat there in front of the box all night and every night.

'We'll go to a restaurant, Joe, maybe, tonight?' she'd say; 'that new place, over by the bridge?' Sometimes with her coat in her hand, running it through her hands, like a kid desperate to be treated – Steve could always remember the piteous sight.

Inevitably, Steve rebelled against his father's advice, as many lads do; Joe wasn't much of an example, sitting by the fire coughing and getting fat. Steve grew a bit, got himself fit and spent some time in the police, where minding your own business inevitably meant minding some other people's as well. Walking into late night drinking dens meant getting involved whether you liked it or not, glasses and fists flying about and some of them out of their minds on God knows what.

The police job suited Steve in a few ways, which included meeting Lyn. She was temping in one of the magistrate's offices he went to frequently; they got talking, and eventually talking properly, seriously, one day when Steve was waiting for a shoplifting case. Very romantic, she would always say. In time, she ran an office herself, and persuaded Steve to leave the police after a case where a policeman was shot dead, following a few other incidents; she wanted a living husband, not a dead hero, she announced to him, her sexy little green eyes flashing. He grumbled a bit, but after a while did as he was told. He started in security, sometimes jobs with dogs, yes, but all pretty safe stuff, gated developments, nobby golf clubs, country club hotels, that kind of thing. And he eventually fetched up in what Lyn would call 'an office job at last,' getting quite decent money for old rope.

Steve concluded fatalistically that the result would be him turning slowly into his dad, until something came along which made him think differently.

Most CCTV security men have their regulars, who are irritating and reassuring at the same time. Cameras on entrances will find people using them for meeting places; on car parks, there will always be someone who regularly turns up in the dead of night or the very early morning, going on or off shift wherever they're working, that kind of thing. It's obvious what they're about, just their daily business, but they have to be watched anyway, because it's known to be the way that some of the big heists come about, deliberately luring security into not watching any more. Regulars get to be like old friends with irritating habits, sitting next to you sniffing and snorting away and never blowing their nose.

One regular in particular Steve didn't get onto until after a few days, mostly because he was the sort of guy who tended to fade into the background; tall but fairly thin, dressed in a sort of anorak thing, a bit pale and pasty, like he hadn't had a good holiday in a while and wouldn't dare strip on the beach if he did. But Steve finally placed him as a boy who used to work in one of the offices, doing what, he couldn't remember, but something pretty junior, since he wasn't that old now. Why he was hanging about the entrance wasn't too clear until Steve got a surprise; a Girl, note the capital G, came up to him.

Steve kept the tapes; they always get kept for a while, at least. Most of the speech was clear enough, and where it's muffled, logic can fill it in.

'Nick, darling, have you been waiting long? Everyone seemed to have business just as I was on my way out.'

'No, Jane, love.' His voice was quieter than hers, and a little quavery. 'Five minutes, no more. I've enjoyed spending a few minutes just looking forward to meeting you.'

She gave him one of those classic girl expressions, along the lines of 'you're a soppy sod, but I love you' and they kissed, full drawn-out tongues job, before heading off together.

After that, it happened more or less the same time everyday, early evening; Steve concluded they were sharing the same car and probably the same flat. Affectionate little chat, big kiss, off they went.

Jane was something else, too, a real treat for the eye, even on the CCTV cameras, a brunette with her hair sweeping down, eyes so bright you could clearly make them out in the camera shot, light blue and alive, really alive. O.K., a bit of God's gift about the way she'd throw her head back and bring her arm up to run down over his cheek like he was a good boy. And he always jolted into life by her just getting there, like a puppy dog jumping up out of its basket.

Steve began to get a bit impatient with it. Always somewhere between 5.30 and 5.45 in the afternoon, when he was on days, Nick would be there, just at the time when paperwork needed finishing off, because not much usually happened at that time, with people just concerned about getting home. But the job meant he had to give Nick an odd glance, standing there blowing on his hands like little boy lost; on Steve's patch, Steve has to watch him. She comes, his tail wags, off they go. Steve found himself mystified to understand what she saw in him, but it wasn't the first time that what women see in their guys puzzled him. What on earth does such a girl want with a skinny anoraked beanpole like Nick, who looked like a good breeze would be enough to blow him away?

But after a while, a greater sympathy set in with his forlorn shape hanging around the entrance until Jane turned up. When it came to rating himself as a partner for her, it looked as if Nick didn't much either, which is not good news in a relationship. Steve could remember so-called friends going on at him when he thought of asking Lyn out – 'leave it out, Steve, you're not in her league, mate,' on and on. Sooner or later, he thought, you have to decide for yourself that you've got enough going for you, because you won't get very far standing in front of them yammering and blushing. If you don't rate yourself, how do you expect women to?

And Nick seemed kind of overwhelmed, buried in the beauty of her. Steve didn't know how long they'd been together before they'd started appearing in his entrance, but he suspected not long. Tensions were starting; sometimes, on the camera, she would give him occasional little twitches of impatience, or grimace at him for saying the wrong thing, and his terror at upsetting her or even getting near to it would show as he almost doubled up as if bowing to her, as if he was shortly about to go down on his knees. Then the old man would return to Steve again; 'you can't live other people's lives for them,' a standard trotted out when he told him he'd joined the police.

The first real trouble between them happened on a Wednesday, Nick's third time there that week. 17.30, he's stood there as usual. Steve got on with his paperwork, observation reports, equipment maintenance, all that stuff. 17.40, he glanced again; Nick's still there. She's gone shopping, pal, Steve thought, she forgot to tell you.

17.47, still there. 18.05, still there. Now he's banging his feet up and down on the pavement, and it isn't all to keep warm, the little squit has a temper after all.

It's just after quarter past six, 18.17, when she turns up. At first, she's apologetic, making little girl faces, holding her lips to his cheek, caressing his neck.

'Something just needed sorting, Nick; I couldn't get away.'

But now the shining is in his eyes, and it's pure anger.

'Bloody hell, Jane. I'm freezing my effing arse off here.'

She physically backs away from him, almost as if he'd hit her. The movements suggested that this wasn't a new routine, it was a scene they'd been through before somewhere else.

'Must you use that language to me?' she says. And she's off, no kiss, no embrace, puppy dog following, pleading with her, his arms wide, his body leaning forward, like a kid trying to talk himself out of punishment.

Sure enough, Thursday she's as late again. But this time, what passes for apology is brisk, abrupt, forestalling the possibility of his objection.

'Work again. Ready? We'll need to shop.'

He holds his hands palm up in front of her and grins - who cares?

'Yes, sure. You got here, that's the main thing. I know it's a busy time at work.'

And that's it. Surrender. No protest, no comment. Fool, fool, fool, Steve thought, those determined to be doormats will have feet wiped all over them alright.

By Friday, Steve was involved, his paperwork suspended, sitting as if waiting for the show. This is the night when all the roads are at their very worst, more need for an early get out of town than any other time. She turns up at half past six. Appeasement out the window now; one long sort of combined snort and snarl

193

and he's stormed off down the road before she even gets to him.

Steve thought, here I am being sympathetic with the guy, in spite of thinking that she's insane to go with the skinny sod in the first place. Maybe she's under pressure at work and she's forced to work late; maybe she's told him that and he's preferring to play the martyr waiting for her.

They weren't there at the weekend, of course, and Steve started thinking what a sad git he was turning into; maybe the old man had a point after all, what the hell's it got to do with him anyway? Then it occurs to him that if something happened in that spot, right near the entrance, security could come into it as far as the companies in the building were concerned. He considered whether he should get down there and move them on, tell them to find somewhere else to meet up.

By Monday, his interest had become professional as well as casual. 5.30, 5.40. 5.50, no sign of either of them. He wondered whether they'd split up, had the final row, moved somewhere else. Time passed; he thought, fair enough, that's that, they've made other arrangements, and no bad thing either. Then she's suddenly there, on her own; definitely her, and the clock on 18.14. She's flustered at him not being there; the colour in her cheeks is visible enough. 18.21, and she's got her arms folded, rigid with temper, elbows sticking out, indifferent to mildly irritated people squeezing past her. Her hands are tightening and untightening against her body, maybe as if she had his neck in her grip.

18.26, she freezes, like a lioness waiting for the kill; she's seen him. He saunters into the picture; he's carrying shopping bags, there's a kind of soppy grin on his face.

For a moment, it really does look like something violent is going to happen; a few passers-by look at her curiously, standing there crimsoned with steam coming out of her head.

'Nick, what the hell is going on?'

The soppy grin slips a little; he puts the bags down very carefully.

'Well, since you get here late and then we have to shop, I thought for once I'd do the shopping first so we can go home at a reasonable time.'

Now her hands have gone down to her hips and she's leaning forward towards him, her body saying that the hands are where they are because she can't trust them not to set about him. She goes off like a firecracker, right there on the pavement.

'You stupid, stupid man! As if you'd know what to bloody shop for! Do you think I enjoy working until God knows when, do you think I'd do it if I could avoid it? You've got the' – her lips form the f sound, she hesitates momentarily, then thinks what the hell, go for it – 'fucking nerve to pull stupid stunts and leave me standing here in the street!' She's off, in any direction as long as it's away from him.

He's paralysed, his hands stock still at his sides; if he isn't crying, he's not far off.

After a few seconds, he kind of concertinas in on himself, his head going down and his right hand coming up to meet it as if someone has just struck him.

And so to Tuesday; Steve finds himself almost waiting for them. This time Nick's there in position and on time. But he's on his own and he stays on his own. As the minutes pass, he's getting unhappier; he looks up at the sky, he looks down and bumps his feet up and down; at one point he squats down and puts his head between his hands.But it's all useless. Steve feels instinctively that she's not coming.

At quarter to seven, he's still there, sitting on the ground now, and one or two people passing obviously think he's some kind of down and out and walk as widely away from him as they can.Steve wonders whether he'll still be there at the change over time, 20.00. But Nick hears the chimes of seven and they seem to jolt movement in him; he's suddenly up and gone like a bolt of lightning had passed through him.

Wednesday, and Steve cannot believe Nick is going to go through it all again. Cut your losses, walk home, whatever, don't put yourself through it. But no, there he is. A little late, 17.43, but there all the same, and a minute or two needed to place him, one because he's wearing a new coat, noticeably smarter than his anorak thing and, two, when Steve bothers to look, he seems altogether a bit tidier, better presented, you might say. 'Son, you're losing the plot,' Steve thinks; as if this is going to be solved with a wash and brush up.

At 18.53, Nick's hands are clasped in front of him like a priest, swaying slightly backwards and forwards. Something about him says big trouble, a catastrophe happening and happening to him, his whole body clenching in on itself.

She's there, but not on her own; a well-dressed, easy-moving older guy is with her, and his coat is much better even than skinny Nick's new one. Though Steve acknowledges that Jane and her new guy look much more of a suited couple, he finds himself appalled at what's happening to the kid right there in the street.

'Nick,' she says, very evenly, but a kind of relish in the voice, 'as you've made so much fuss about my overtime, I thought you might like to meet him.'

196

Old Smoothie smiles and there's even the ghost of a chuckle. Steve's face is almost pressed against the screen now, and yes, those are tears running down Nick's cheeks, and his arms are clutched across his guts like someone's just hoofed him. Sat on the ground, he looks now like the kid he essentially is, lanky and outsized for both age and ambition. Jane's suitor, probably also her boss, I would guess, has turned away now; perhaps he's not a complete shit, Steve thinks.

She moves across to Nick very carefully, as if sidling up to a sleeping lunatic. She touches his shoulder very lightly; remorse, compensation, some kindly intention. He twists his right arm up in a sudden jolt, as if her fingers were white hot, and his arm stays raised in the air. He's looking at her, and while Steve can't see the details of the look, it's clearly hitting her like a push; she's backing right across the pavement away from him and bumping into new older man, who grabs the moment, and her, to make off; enough is enough.

He's still half doubled up. A middle-aged lady hesitates and then moves towards him; he shakes his head and holds his hands up and she backs reluctantly away. For two more minutes he stands there, now leaning side on against the wall to conceal what he's doing.

Then he moves away, but not gone to his right, as he always has done before, he's gone off to the left, down the alley leading to the car park which serves this office block and only this office block.

With a rising fear, Steve wonders what the hell is he doing, and the realisation arrives that effectively he's not out there in the neutral big, outside world any longer, he's now in the office's inner security space, and therefore he's not a story going on out there, he's a problem – Steve's problem. Steve checks the car park monitor, thinking if he's gone down that alley, he's got to finish up in the car park or reappear passing the entrance. He doesn't.

Now Steve has a cold sweat on the back of his palm and he flicks back to check the internal stairs; there he is, making his way up them as if he's entered stair running as an Olympic event. Thin frame, new coat, him without a doubt. Someone has left that bloody fire door open again and Nick has remembered it happens. Steve makes a mental note to create hell this time, but now, action needs taking very urgently, because rocket science is not needed to work out what it is he's trying to do. Everyone knows the roof garden on this place, especially people who've worked here before; nice easy little jumping off wall around it. And he wouldn't be the first one.

The roof garden door is no more than twenty yards from Steve's door, but he only just makes it before Nick; no sooner has he locked his own door behind him than he's aware of Nick, half way up the final stairs before the top, close enough to give off an aroma of the cool night air and the brand new cloth of his coat. Skinny he is, yes, but there's much, much more of him than there is on a monitor screen and he is on the very edge.

'Unlock that door, unlock it now, just do it.'

'No can do, pal. Security.'

'What the hell do you mean, security? It's a fucking roof garden.'

'Private roof garden. Sorry. Can't be done.'

'I want air. I feel sick. Just open the fucking door!'

He's very red now, still panting after the stairs, but not panting very much; he's a large, fit young guy in his mid-twenties and he is, at this moment, insane, his eyes blazing with anger and tears. Steve is forty-six and doesn't like to think of himself as decrepit, but he doesn't run many marathons or take much care of his fitness any more. Like it or not, he is involved up to his neck and might well be getting a good kicking any moment now.

Nick goes off pop suddenly and absolutely, his face contorting into a grimace of intense pain, someone already having done to him what he wants to do to Steve, and he literally takes off from the step he's on direct at Steve, who gets very, very lucky; his right fist is coming up hard and hopefully and it connects heavily against the side of the younger man's head with a noise like snapped wood. He's down and his head clatters against the concrete next to the stairs, then, unconscious, he clunks on down the staircase. He's lying there at the bottom of the stairs like a great grotesque skinny doll, arms spread out and legs twisted almost up into his chest. For one frozen moment Steve fears Nick is actually dead, then his arm gives an involuntary twitch and Steve goes down to feel the pulse; still quite strong, but no way of knowing for how long. Steve knows not to try and move him and phones an ambulance just as a couple of guys from the nearest office arrive, all consideration and consternation, like they haven't been parking themselves strategically in the background until they see whether the madman manages to rip Steve's head off.

The ambulance guys arrive in ten minutes, and in the meantime, Steve watches Nick carefully without being too sure exactly what to do if he suddenly seemed worse.

As they put Nick on the stretcher, he starts to wake up. He looks so lost, like a

bewildered kid; he reminds Steve physically of his own lad David, though David is now no longer a lad and certainly no longer bewildered. Nick doesn't know where or who he is, so Steve squeezes his hand and smiles at him, and believes it is probably the first time Nick hasproperly registered his existence as another human being. Nick stares for some time, maybe already wanting

199

to apologise but just not having even the minute amount of energy needed to do that.

Now Steve checks with the ambulance guys as to where they're taking him and goes to visit the hospital the next day. Having been through a fair bit to save this guy's life, Nick has become a kind of investment and Steve wants to know more about what kind of life it was he'd saved. Nick already looks much better, and at close quarters, the skinniness becomes a bit of an illusion at a distance because of his height – he must be about 6'3". He is bruised here and there and recovering from concussion and shock. For about the first ten minutes, he won't stop apologising and kind of putting himself down as mad, crazy, off his head etc., and Steve's sympathy with Jane grows by the minute; in some ways, he prefers the fire-breathing young colossus stood on the steps below him the day before. For once, talking in hospital is easy; Steve wants to know more about him, not least because he doesn't fancy having to fight him off his roof again.

Steve puts up with it for about quarter of an hour, then decides what to do; perhaps not what a counsellor or doctor would recommend, but he knew he was going to do it anyway, because apart from anything else, he considers himself owed. He gets up as if about to go, but actually uses the standing position as more comfortable for saying what he wants to say.

'Nick, you know how many times you said 'I used to' do this, that and the other? You used to be in the athletics club doing distance running; you used to like swimming; you stopped both because she didn't like either of them much and they took up too much time and money. You climbed a bit, and then she didn't like you taking the risk. Let me tell you something; I don't claim to be the most expert agony aunt in the world, but I know enough to see a difference between relationships and doormats. If you want a mistress to kiss the feet of and crawl to occasionally, go to someone professional, don't live your whole life like it. It's not fair either to you or the girl. Don't keep telling yourself you're such a useless article when you're obviously alright with at least two sports and guys are prepared to risk their lives with you on the other end of a climbing rope. If all you can do is put yourself down, son, that's all everyone else is likely to do.'

Steve stops as he realises he is almost shouting and on the end of a very dirty look from a passing nurse. He reflects that one or two expletives may have crept in to his speech. He looks down and sees, to his astonishment, Nick grinning like his face might split. He can think of nothing better to do than wink and walk off.

Weeks passed; Steve stops thinking about the whole business. He has enough on his plate, and wherever they were, Nick and Jane, they weren't meeting up on his patch and that suited him fine.

But about three months later, well into the summer, on the verge of a changeover, he sees someone actually waving into the camera from the front entrance. Cheeky sod, he thinks at first. After a minute or two, he recognises Nick; the guy has filled out a bit and he's dressed for a night on the town.

There's a girl with him, a pretty redhead, about his age; she's looking at him half amazed, half amused, but with a look that says frankly enough that she fancies him. He does a big elaborate bow to the camera, then a quick thumbs up. They wander off, but Steve can't leave it at that. He dashes out on to the roof garden to wave and shout.

'Nick! Have a good night, mate!' he shouts down the road.

201

Nick turns right round and spreads his arms wide, like it's a big, beautiful world, and the girl's on him, eyes and questions.

Steve stands enjoying the fresh air for a while, until he can hear Harry coming up the stairs for the changeover. Sorry Dad, he thinks, dear old Dad minding his own to the last, a final cigarette and dead in his chair, almost unnoticed for a while. I suppose I just can't help minding someone else's now and then, if and when they obviously need it to be minded. That's the way I am, Dad, and that's the way I'll stay.